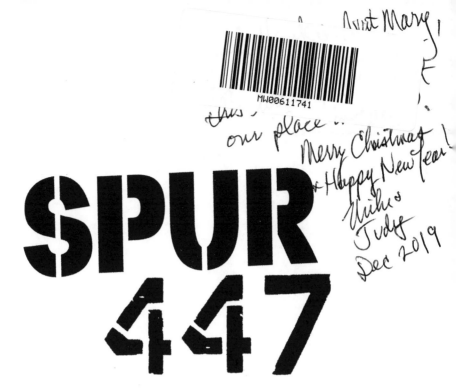

Aunt Mary!

this our place..

Merry Christmas & Happy New Year!

Mike & Judy

Dec 2019

SPUR 447

SPUR 447

A NOVEL

Michael K. Birkmeier

ISBN: 978-0-578-60257-8

Doc with Lady B, circa 1968

This book is for the family and friends, past, present, and future, of that old schoolhouse cabin just outside of Trout Lake, Michigan.

CONTENTS

FOREWORD

The idea for *Spur 447* happened about ten years ago while I was deer hunting at our cabin in Michigan's Upper Peninsula. You see, there really aren't many deer in the UP, so your mind tends to wander as you sit in your blind, waiting for some action, and that's where I dreamed up the idea for this story. Eventually, I was compelled to put it on paper, but getting started was an overwhelming endeavor because I am an engineer by trade, not a writer. However, with some persistence, the words started to flow, and two years later, the manuscript was finally completed!

So, I should tell you more about our cabin. It's located just outside of Trout Lake and has been in the family since the late forties, purchased by my grandpa and three of his friends. My grandpa's name was Francis, and he was an osteopathic physician. They called him Doc, for obvious reasons. The cabin is an old schoolhouse, build in the early 1900s. It has aged well, all things considered. The cedar siding is weathered and curled, but the structure and foundation are sound, and the roof doesn't leak. For our family, it's a place that holds many special memories—many even documented on the walls! The cabin has no electricity or running water. Copper tubing snakes overhead, delivering propane for gas lamps, while an old fuel oil heater warms the rooms. The walls are peppered with antler mounts, photos, scribblings, and all sorts of knick-knacks (probably too much of them). But best of all, the cabin is located across the road from the old Soo Line railway, where trains continue to rumble by the schoolhouse two or three times a day and rattle the glass in the windows. The experience is exhilarating, especially when the train rolls through at two in the morning!

In the end, writing this book turned out to be a wonderful experience, as family and friends willingly supplied information about its characters and events, which gave the story depth. Thanks to them, the story came to life effortlessly. Two people who provided countless tidbits of information were Pete Schwesinger and Tim Lyman, who damn near "wrote" a couple of chapters for me. I would also like to thank Tom Rademacher for reviewing my manuscript, offering improvements, providing insight into the editing and publishing process, and encouraging me to proceed with this endeavor. I was overwhelmed with emotion from Tom's wonderful comments about my initial manuscript. They gave me confirmation that I had written something special. Much thanks to my son, Chris, who deftly suggested how to get past writer's block when I hit those snags. Author Steve Hamilton gets props for his Alex McKnight series, which take place in Paradise, Michigan, just up the road from Trout Lake. His books were the impetus for me to start writing. Special thanks to Rachel Paul and Lotus Editing and Design. It was so satisfying to watch her take my manuscript and cover concept and transform it into something truly wonderful. An experienced jack-of-all-trades, from editing to self-publishing, Rachel was a delight to work with and understood what this book meant to me. And finally, thanks to my wife Judy for being a sounding board as I bugged her endlessly about my ideas and wrote the manuscript. Her never-ending love and support kept me going.

So, why don't you get comfortable, grab your favorite beverage, and turn the page? I hope that you enjoy reading this book as much as I enjoyed writing it!

Mike

ABOUT THE AUTHOR

Mike Birkmeier is a Chief Operating Officer for a small manufacturing firm in Grandville,
Michigan. Outside of work, he
enjoys spending time with his
family, especially with his lovely
wife of thirty-one years, Judy.
Mike considers himself blessed to
have a wonderful group of family and friends and enjoys their
never-ending gatherings. He also
enjoys college football, golfing,

running, biking, hiking, traveling, cooking (and eating), and
hunting. Mike and Judy have three amazing children, Chris,
Sarah, and Stephanie, and reside in Belmont, Michigan.

CHAPTER 1

THE MIGHTY MAC

Here comes the big bend. For some reason, that's what I call it. Just past mile marker 332 on northbound I-75, south of Mackinaw City. In a couple of minutes, as the highway straightens north, I'll see the Mighty Mac—the Mackinaw Bridge. The gateway into Michigan's Upper Peninsula, or what we Michiganders call the UP. It's the fifth longest suspension bridge in the world, connecting the Upper Peninsula to Michigan's lower mainland. The magnificent bridge bisects Lake Michigan on the west and Lake Huron on the east. As I complete the long turn, the bridge slowly appears, with both suspension cables lit the entire length with lights. They used the lights during construction back in the fifties, and it looked so spectacular that they left them on. Angled slightly to the right, you can see the arch of the roadway as it reaches north, from Mackinaw City to St. Ignace, dotted with headlights moving slowly in both directions. The sight of the bridge makes the hairs on my arms stand up every time I see it.

1

The flashing road sign near the Jamet Street exit in Mackinaw City declares to motorists: *High Wind Warning— Tune to AM 530.* Looks like they are escorting any high-risk vehicles tonight. It sure would be a bummer to get blown off the side of this thing. I recall that back in the late eighties, someone actually did go over the side (in a blue Yugo, no less): a girl from Royal Oak, in her early thirties, on her way to meet someone in St. Ignace. She lost control of the tiny car on the bridge; veered into oncoming traffic; and then darted back across the northbound lane, slamming into the curb. It slid along the outer rail for about 40 feet before hitting one of the support cables and then flipped over the side, falling 170 feet before hitting the water. The event turned into a media circus because the car took more than a week to locate. The poor girl's remains were still inside the crumpled car when they found it. The police report said that she was driving more than sixty miles per hour, which, along with the high winds, contributed to the accident. Hence the warning sign, and why the Bridge Authority recommends speeds less than twenty miles per hour during high wind events. Oh shoot! I promised to call my wife! I voice the phone commands into the vehicle's Bluetooth, and it rings.

"Hey Jude, how you doing?"

"Not too bad," she says. "Missing you already, though! Where are you?"

I think about the high wind warning and wonder if I should tell her I'm about ready to cross the bridge.

"I'm just starting to cross the bridge. Figured I would give you a call before I lose the cell signal on the other side. You know, Verizon covers 99 percent of the nation, but not the UP."

She laughs. "Well, I'm glad you called to let me know you made it. It's still really windy here. Is it bad up there?"

Ah shit, I knew she would ask.

"Well, yeah, it's windy. The warning sign's flashing, so they are escorting the at-risk vehicles. You know the routine. Not a problem, though. I'll just take it easy and drive slow."

I know she doesn't like that I am crossing in high winds, but it really doesn't bother me. I've done it a bunch of times.

"You know the wind makes me nervous crossing that bridge. Be careful!"

I can hear the tension in her voice…time to change the subject, real quick. "Yeah, I will. It's no big deal. Hey, did you see that Michigan State won?"

She perked up. "Yeah, I watched the last half. They beat Rutgers pretty bad, so I didn't have to rub my nuts."

I laugh out loud. Judy has this necklace made of green-and-white painted nuts. I think they are Hawaiian kukui nuts. Big suckers. Anyways, she has this superstitious habit of rubbing those nuts to give the Spartans good luck when they need some. You can only imagine the creative comments made by our friends as we watch her rub them during a game!

"Well, that's a good thing. So, hey, I'm going to let you go. Just wanted to check in and tell you I got to the bridge, safe and sound. I'll try to call or text you in a few days, if I can get a signal."

"Oh, alright. Have fun up there and I hope you catch a deer!"

Why does she always say "catch" a deer? We shoot them.

"Yeah, OK. I'll make sure to catch a deer, honey. I love you!"

"I love you too, Mikey!"

I put the phone down and admire the bridge. It's amazing as always. The lights on the suspension cables look so cool at night. I sneak a peek up at the first tower as I drive under it. At the midpoint, I pass a big semi-rig driving slowly, escort truck in front, amber lights flashing. My tires immediately start to sing as I get into the left lane, which is constructed of open metal grating. The tires howl in different pitches as the car passes over each section, like a song. During the day, you can catch glimpses of the water below. Creepy, for sure. Eventually, I pass the two twenty-four-inch-diameter suspension cables where they descend and terminate into the north suspension anchor point. I reach for my wallet and grab a five-dollar bill.

A mile or so later, the toll booth approaches. As the vehicles ahead pay the tolls and drive on, I can see one of the booth attendants. Yep, looks like the same Native American guy I have seen for years. I wonder which tribe he might belong to— Chippewa or Ottawa? The man is always so polite. As I pull up, I put my window down and he leans out of the booth a bit and greets me kindly.

"Good evening, sir. How you doing tonight?"

I smile back. "Pretty darn good, now that the Spartans finally won a football game. Beat Rutgers on the road pretty bad this evening, forty-nine to zip. Hard to believe they only have three wins."

I hand him the five spot.

He nods his head. "Yeah, I heard. They needed that. Big news up here is St. Ignace High won last night. We play Muskegon Catholic Central next Friday. I hear they have a pretty good team, but our kids are pumped. I think we are good enough to get to the state finals."

Yeah, good luck with that one, I think to myself. UP kids are pretty tough, but I'm not convinced they can compete with the city kids from Muskegon. I'll have to ask him how they did on the trip home if I see him again.

"Well, good luck to your team, and have a wonderful weekend!" I say.

He gives me my change and asks me if I am up to hunt. I nod with a smile, and he wishes me good luck. He mentions that the deer herd is coming back, so we might see a few more this year. Good news. I hit the gas and settle back into my seat. Thirty more minutes, and I'll be there.

As the first exit approaches, a decision looms. Do I head west on US-2 to the Shell station and pick up some feed, or should I just get it at Mel's South-Side in Trout Lake tomorrow? If my son, Chris, was with me, we would stop for sure, get some gas, pick up some feed, and he would buy a package of red licorice. I wonder if he will ever make it back up here, now that he is in Los Angeles. I know he loved it up here. Maybe one of these days, after he makes it big as a movie director, he can fly into St. Ignace, and I can pick him up on the way through.... Suddenly, I realize that I'm driving westbound on US-2. I chuckle to myself. Must be the licorice.

I pull in and park next to an open stall at the gas station. A half-dozen vehicles are getting gas, shuffling through the station. It's pretty busy for a Saturday night. I get out of the vehicle, slide a credit card through the reader, and place the nozzle into the tank. Strolling past the bumper while I wait, I gaze south toward the water, close my eyes, and take in a deep breath. The calming smell of the lake is all around, and a wave of relaxation spreads through me. It's so good to be back! I love coming up here. My dad always said that in the UP, your troubles melt away and your worries disappear. He was right. I feel it every time I come up here, and I felt it long before he even mentioned that to me. I completely understand the feeling, and I'm sure my grandpa and his buddies felt it too. I can't help but smile.

The headlights from a champagne-colored Lincoln SUV grab my attention as it pulls in and parks in front of me. Illinois license plate. The driver's door swings open, and a leg appears covered in pressed khakis, sporting a nicely polished boot. An older gentleman in his mid- to late sixties gets out, wearing a smart-looking tan upland jacket and a brown Stetson. He looks in my direction, tips his hat, and says hello. I start to reply back but can't get the words out. I just stare at him, dumfounded. Holy shit, he looks just like grandpa—white goatee and all!

"Hey, you OK over there?" he asks, laughing just a bit.

"Oh, yeah, sure. Good evening. Sorry about that," I finally blurt out.

"You were standing there with your eyes closed, smiling, when I drove up."

"Yeah, I was. I love the smell of the air right here. It's the lake. The fishiness. The sand. The moisture."

"I know what you mean. Your worries just melt away, right?"

"Exactly! I was just thinking that!"

He laughs again and nods his head in agreement as he twists off his gas cap.

"You heading north to hunt?" he asks, swiping his credit card through the reader.

"Sure am, how about you?" I say, squinting to get a better look at this feller.

"Yep. Headed to Paradise to meet up with a couple of old friends. They have a cabin there, with lots of land to hunt. I'm pretty excited. Used to come up here all of the time, but it's been forty years since the last time."

"Wow, that's a big gap! What happened?"

"Life happened, I guess. Sometimes, along the way, you forget about the things that are important. But eventually, you figure it out."

There seems to be some melancholy in his voice.

"But hey, I'm glad to be making the trip up again. Actually, I'm excited as hell."

"I bet your buddies are glad you're coming. Forty years… Are you expecting it to be different?"

"Oh, I'm sure it will be. Heck, the drive up was different than what I remember. I stopped in Cheboygan at a place where we always used to eat, and it was no longer there!"

"That's unfortunate. What was it called?"

"Carnation. Have the best steaks around! Or…*had* the best steaks around. I was looking forward to having my usual, the Chicago Steak. Big as a bus and melts in your mouth."

The Carnation? I'll be damned. That's the place where my grandpa and his buddies would stop on the way to the cabin! The stories of their trips to that restaurant were legendary. What are the odds that I would run into someone who looks like my grandpa, is also from Illinois, and knows about the Carnation?

I keep my composure as a flood of memories and questions arise in my mind. "I've heard of it but didn't know it was closed. Never been there, but my grandpa and his buddies would always stop there, too."

"They did have a reputation for good steaks. I can still see it, in big red letters: Carnation—The House of Chicago Steaks," he says, simulating the marquee with his hand gliding through the air.

Click. The pump stops, and I replace the nozzle and screw in the gas cap. Receipt in hand, I walk over to get a closer look at my grandpa's doppelganger.

"My name's Mike. Nice to meet you," I say, reaching out to shake his hand.

"Nice to meet you, Mike. Name's Frank," he replies, shaking my hand with a nice, strong grip.

Up close, his resemblance to my grandpa is comfortably eerie—Stetson, goatee, the shape of his nose and eyes, the droopy earlobes, and the way he is dressed. Oh and let's not forget the nice shoes. *And* he's driving a Lincoln. Grandpa always drove nice cars. Jags. Cadillacs. Lincolns.

I laugh, then say, "You're not a doctor, are you?"

Frank smiles warmly, then says, "Nope. Lawyer. Why do you ask?"

I chuckle and shake my head.

"You just remind me of a doctor who I knew—that's all. His name was Francis."

Click. The pump stops, and Frank pulls the nozzle, replaces the cap, and grabs the receipt.

"Francis…nice name." He smiles. "Well, Mike, it was wonderful meeting you," he says, gently patting me on the shoulder, "Oh, what's your destination?"

"Trout Lake. We have a cabin there, just west of town."

"I know Trout Lake. My buddies and I would typically stop there for a few beers on the way to Paradise."

"It's a small town—don't blink, or you'll miss it," I say.

Frank laughs. "You got that right! Well, drive safe, and good luck hunting."

"Yeah, you too. And I hope everything is as good as it was forty years ago."

He smiles, and confirms with a nod, "I'm sure it will be. I can feel it in my bones."

We shake hands, exchange smiles, and part ways. I head into the store and grab a bag of red licorice.

As I stroll back to my car, the Lincoln is gone. What a nice guy, and what a pleasant conversation. Back on the road, I head east on US-2 and take the exit for I-75 north, toward Sault Ste. Marie. I can't stop thinking about my grandpa.

Ten minutes later, I take the Moran exit and head north on M-123. Twenty more minutes and I'll be at the cabin. I tune the radio to ESPN sports and get the rundown on today's college football games. Gosh, what a relief—Michigan State won. Only three wins so far, just one year after reaching the college football playoffs. Nobody saw this coming. Maybe they can finish the season strong by winning the last two games. I set my cruise control to sixty and find myself in a trance watching the road go by. There are no other cars in sight. It's so desolate up here—vast amounts of land where nobody goes. I once heard the UP is one-third of Michigan's total land area, with only 3 percent of the overall population. I can see why Judy gets freaked out when we take road trips up here. It's not unusual to drive for a half hour and not see a single car. What the heck would you do if the car broke down? No cell phone reception. Not a good situation.

I pass through Moran, and then after fifteen more minutes, I spot the lights from Mel's South-Side, just outside of Trout Lake. Driving through town, I pass a few parked cars in front of the Trout Lake Bar and the Buck Rub. Lo and behold—a champagne-colored Lincoln SUV with Illinois plates is parked out front. I shake my head and smile, passing on the urge to stop and have a beer with Frank. The magnetic pull of the cabin is too strong. I turn left on H-40, drive over the twin sets of railroad tracks, and head west. The tracks parallel the left side of the road as I drive out of town. Two more miles. OJ Miller Road approaches on the left. One more mile. Then, I see it— the faint glow of propane lights coming through the windows of the old schoolhouse. I slow down, turn right on Wilwin Road, and then make a quick right again in the yard, behind the cabin. Pete mowed for us. Nice! We'll have to have him and

Sonja over for dinner one night. Pete is the son of Charles Jr. and Lanie Schweitzer. Charlie died some years back, but Lanie still lives across the street. Pete's sister, Laurie, and her husband, Rod, also live next door. The Schweitzer clan owns quite a bit of property around our camp, some of which we hunt on. Pete's dad and his siblings actually attended the schoolhouse that is now our cabin.

Looks like my brother, Dave, is here, along with Tim, Kent, and, I'll be damned, Kerry! Who else would drive a Mustang to deer camp? After parking the car, I reach over to the passenger seat, grab my felt Stetson, and put it on. It's eleven o'clock, and the evening is crisp and clear. As I get out of the car, my eyes wander to the stars. You can see so many of them—no light pollution up here. It is so awesome. Turning, I take two steps up to the porch, twist the doorknob, and enter the century-old schoolhouse. I peek around the corner to see four smiling faces.

CHAPTER 2

HOMECOMING

"Hey guys! How you doing?"

Tim, Kent, Dave, and Kerry each greet me with hugs and handshakes.

"Damn, it's nice and warm in here!" I say.

"Everything fired right up, just like we were here yesterday," says Tim, with a tumbler of Crown in one hand and an antique car magazine in the other.

"When did you get up here?"

"Kent and I got here around 3:00 p.m. Took our time. Stopped at Bell's in Mackinaw City and got some smoked fish. No car issues this time!"

That's a relief—a few years ago when Tim was headed up with Kent late one night, the water pump went out on his 1975 Chevy Suburban. If I recall correctly, they finally got here at about two in the morning. They had to talk some old geezer into opening up his parts store to get a replacement pump. Then they had to install it in the dark!

"Kerry, glad you could make it up here! How long you staying?"

"Probably Wednesday. Got to get back after that."

Kerry has a job that he really loves. He works at Ford and drives prototypes on the test track. He is pretty much known as the guy who troubleshoots performance issues. He can take a car for a spin, tell the engineers exactly what's wrong, and tell them how to fix it. Unfortunately, his job was so demanding that he was never home with his family. A few years ago, his wife packed up, took the kids, and left him. That fall, when he came up to hunt, he couldn't find the clip to his .30-06. He thinks that his wife was advised by her lawyer to toss all gun ammo prior to serving him the divorce papers. And that's likely what she did—including the clips. Kerry claims he remembered taking the garbage out that week. It felt real heavy—so heavy that he wondered what the hell was in there. I guess he found out that fall when he couldn't find his ammo and clips.

"Hey, nice Mustang out there, Kerry. What's under the hood?"

"Four-cylinder turbo. 310 horses. Kicks some ass."

"Damn, maybe we can take it for a spin later?"

"Sure, no problem!" Kerry says, grinning devilishly at that suggestion. The dude likes to drive fast, so I'm sure that I will get a pretty good ride.

Kent is sitting in the corner, looking at one of the vintage *Playboy* magazines. Kent and Tim have been friends for quite a few years. He has been coming up regularly with Tim for the last decade or so. He is our resident expert on everything. Ask him a question, and he knows the answer. Really, he does.

Unfortunately, Kent knows so much that it can backfire on him. For example, a few years ago, when cougar sightings were a passing fancy in Trout Lake, Kent was chock full of cougar attack facts. He would tell us stories of how hikers in California are attacked, dragged into the woods, partially eaten, and eventually found by someone hiking a few days later. He was especially specific on their preferred method of attack, which was to ambush the victims overhead from the trees. The hikers never had a chance. Anyways, Pete was over one night, and he tells us that his son Charlie was driving west on H-40, about a couple of miles west of camp. A deer crossed the road, so he slowed down. Then, seemingly out of nowhere, this cougar leaps across the road, chasing after the deer. He told his dad that the cougar leaped from the snow bank, to the middle of the road, then onto the other snow bank. Two hops. Scared the hell out of Charlie. So the next morning, Kent and I are walking out to our blinds—the fourth day in a row, to be exact. It's about six, dark as heck, and we have our headlamps on. Kent keeps tripping behind me, which is not a comforting thought, since he's carrying a loaded high-powered rifle. His headlamp keeps flashing up into the trees. So I ask him what the hell is going on, and he tells me that he is looking for cougars because they hide in the trees. For four days we had been trekking out there in the dark before sunrise, and not once was he worried about a cougar attack. Then he hears *one* story about Charlie sighting a cougar two miles from the cabin, and he freaks out!

"Hey Kent, you're looking pretty good—except for that scruffy deer camp beard. I'll bet those girls in that magazine have more hair than you!"

Everybody laughs.

Kent smiles and turns the magazine around, showing everyone Miss May 1970.

"Yep, I guess you're right!"

More laughter from the group.

"So, Tim, did you make the trip to Hershey this year?"

Tim is into all kinds of antiques, especially cars, and takes a trip to Hershey, Pennsylvania, every October for the Antique Auto Show. Kent usually goes with him, along with three or four other guys.

"Yeah, we did. But next year, those other guys can find their own rides and make their own hotel arrangements. It's a hassle to coordinate because everyone is so damn picky, but they don't help plan anything. Then all they do is complain about whatever I set up. So screw 'em."

"That's too bad. Did you take that old motor home down that you bought a few years ago?"

"No, I sold it in the spring. I had to put a new engine in it because the block was cracked." I vaguely recalled that story—something about the only way to remove the engine was to go through the driver's side door. I'm sure he still made a profit, even with the cost of a replacement engine sunk into it.

Tim has been the patriarch of the deer camp group for the last few years. His older brother, Del, hasn't been able to make it up here for various reasons, and my Uncle Bill (who formerly played that role) passed away four years ago. The number of guys coming up for deer season every year has fluctuated, but this year should be pretty good—a total of six if Del's son, Dave, makes it up.

I wonder what it was like back in the days when my grandpa was coming up here. He died in seventy-six, when I was twelve years old. I never really had any conversations with him about his adventures up here. Doc, as they called him, bought this old schoolhouse with Tim's grandpa, Mott, along with two other guys, from a man named Schaar in forty-eight. The Big Mac didn't exist back then, so they had to take the ferry across. I guess Doc was quite a character. He drove around the west side of Lake Michigan one time because he didn't want to wait for the ferry. Rumor has it Doc knew every roadside diner along the way. He always drove nice cars, and according to Tim, always wore expensive shoes. The fourth generation of the original members are coming up here now, and the official membership is at nine. The place gets used in the fall for bird hunting, hiking, and deer hunting. Years ago, it got used fairly often for snowmobiling. My brother, Dave, his buddies, and Uncle Bill would come up nearly every weekend.

"Hey Dave, when did you get here?"

Dave is sitting in the corner, fiddling with some plumbing fixtures and a section of PVC pipe.

"Oh, about nine. I didn't work today, but by the time I finished packing everything up and got the quad loaded, it was later than planned. Then I had to stop in Gaylord to get some food."

"Oh boy, how much food are we going to have this year?"

Everyone in the room laughs! Each year we email back and forth about a meal plan and who's responsible for what. But it never works like it should. Two dozen eggs turn into four dozen. A couple packages of sausage turn into ten. Nobody follows the plan—but what fun would that be? Tim is one of the biggest offenders, and I think that Kent is turning into his apprentice. Last year, he brought up a slab of corn beef brisket that lasted the entire week and screwed up all of the other meal plans.

Dave fires back, "Well, based on the events of the last couple of years, I brought up one loaf of bread, a couple sticks of butter, and one beer."

Everyone laughs again.

I squint in the dim, propane-lit room, trying to see what he is doing.

"What you working on there?"

"Going to replace those valves over the sink. They leak so bad, the pump keeps coming on every five minutes to repressurize the system."

Dave is one of those guys who is always fixing something, since it's never good enough for his liking. He's always tearing something apart, just to see how it works, and then putting it back together. It's no surprise that he's an engineer at Ford. And this old schoolhouse is in pretty good shape, much to Dave's credit. The valves that he is working on connect to an on-demand hot-water system that he and Uncle Bill installed about twenty years ago. It runs on a twelve-volt battery, which trickle charges from a small solar panel. In the past, we had to boil water for dishes, washing up, and what have you. Not now. We just fill up the old ten-gallon milk can, and presto, we get hot water at the sink! They even installed a shower in the back room. Doesn't get used much, though. Dave and Uncle Bill spent quite a bit of time up here in the eighties and nineties, renovating the place. They installed a false ceiling, tore down the old sagging addition, and erected a new section with a wall-mounted propane heater. They also installed an "indoor" outhouse, ran new copper for the propane lights, and built a deck out front. It's actually pretty nice. Doc and his buddies, long past, would be proud that the cabin was still standing and getting used.

Tim stands up. "Do you need a hand unloading?"

"Yeah, that would be nice. Let's get it done so I can grab something to drink."

We both walk outside, and Kent follows. We grab my gear out of the car and put it on the bed I normally sleep in while I'm up here.

"Is your nephew coming up?" I ask Tim.

"Yeah, I'm pretty sure. I don't think he will be here until tomorrow morning, though. Something to do with work and a meeting. He is planning to stay until next Saturday with me and Kent. When are you heading back?"

"I think I am going to head back on Thursday. We have plans Friday in Lansing with some friends, and then we are going to the Michigan State game on Saturday."

"Those Spartans aren't doing so well this year, are they?" says Kent.

"No, they are having a rough year for sure."

I get my sleeping bag unrolled on the bed and put my duffle bag next to it. I place my shotgun and rifle in the gun cabinet. Kent is already established in one front-corner bunk, and Kerry has the other. We are the only ones in the front section. My brother and Tim have their own rooms. Seniority. Finally, I put my cooler on the front porch, grab a beer, and head back inside. It's now eleven thirty.

"So what's the plan for tomorrow? You guys going to do some scouting and get your blinds set up?"

Tim says, "That's the plan. We really didn't have much time to do anything today. Oh yeah, I brought up a couple bags of sugar beets for everyone to use."

Kent adds, "I'm going to hunt an area off Huckleberry, about a half mile to the east, past the bend. They have been doing some logging there, and I can follow the path back to the south."

"I know what you're talking about. We saw that this fall, bird hunting over there."

I recall inspecting the logging equipment with Dave. A huge mechanical beast that grabs trees, cuts them down, saws them into sections, and spits them off to the side, in one smooth motion.

"Dave, you want to go into town tomorrow, and get some corn and apples at Mel's?"

"Yeah, that sounds good."

I look at Kerry.

"Where do you plan to hunt?"

"I might go back to where I missed that buck a few years ago. Are you still hunting around there?"

"Yeah, but I will be further back to the south. We can walk in together. I think that the deer are moving from the swamp south of me, over to you. It will be nice to have a few people hunting there. I saw some deer last year, and Kent did too. Did you bring up a blind?"

"No, we'll just make one."

Dave looks up from the plumbing fixtures.

"That shouldn't take us long at all. We can fix mine up too."

We continue catching up for another hour or so, and then, one by one, we start to head for the bunks.

CHAPTER 3

THE TRAIN

I awaken from a dream and hear it. The train horn, coming from the west, probably going through Rexton, eight miles away. Two long blasts and one short one. Crossing the road, giving the warning signal. I keep listening, and eventually I can hear the drone of the diesel engines, faintly echoing through the woods.

I'm not sure why, but the train is like an old friend stopping by for a visit. It's the remnants of the Soo Line, still running two or three times a day, carrying lumber and taconite pellets across the UP. Back in the day, Trout Lake was a major rail hub in the UP.

The diesels are getting louder now, humming slightly out of synchronization. I look out the window and see lights dancing through the trees—getting closer, moving pretty fast, I think. Two long blasts and one short. The train is approaching Huckleberry, right across the street. As the engine roars past, the cabin literally shakes. Window glass in the century-old schoolhouse rattles in the panes. The wheels make a click-clack sound as they cross the road. There goes a squeaky wheel! I look out the window and see the train barreling toward town, the locomotives leading the way with the lights flickering in the trees. Finally, the last car goes by, with a red blinking light on the hitch. Oscar! For some reason, that's what Uncle Billy called it. Never did ask him why. I watch the red light blink until it disappears.

I think about Judy coming up here for the first time, warning her about the train coming through in the middle of the night, and that it's probably going to scare the shit out of her! The first train is always the best, but all of them are magical. Oddly enough, after the first couple nights, you sleep right through them. Then, the only thing that wakes you up is having to take a leak. I never did figure out why I pee so much in the middle of the night up here. Maybe the beer drinking in the evening? Must have been a common problem, though, because all the old boys joke about having to get up in the middle of the night to go. Probably prostate issues! I'm sure that's why a couple of bedpans hang from hooks on the wall. When my dad's up here, he always commandeers an old coffee can. That way, he can roll right over in bed and go. Fortunately, I haven't lowered myself to that process.

I finally get out of bed and put on my slippers on. Will it be the outhouse or the stars? I opt for the stars. While relieving myself, I gaze upward, still amazed by just how many there are. I finish up, head back in, and climb back into my sleeping bag. Getting comfortable, I drift back to sleep, hoping that I don't have to get up and do this again.

CHAPTER 4

THE FIRST MORNING

I wake up to the hiss-pop sound of propane lights igniting in the kitchen and then hear water pouring into the percolator. From my bed, I see Tim in his baggy long johns and old-school slippers, getting the coffee ready.

"Way to go, Tim!"

"You bet! I just need to get it perking. We should have coffee in about ten minutes. How did you sleep?"

"Pretty good. Only got up to pee one time, right after the train went by. How did you sleep?"

"Great. I heard the train too. Seemed like a long one, coming from Rexton. I had to go also—before the train, though. Hey, did you see the stars last night? Man, were they bright! You could see the Milky Way across the entire sky."

"Yeah, I know. Almost didn't go outside. I always get a bit freaked out there in the middle of the night. I keep thinking coyotes and wolves are going to jump out from the pines!"

Tim chuckles. "Or maybe cougars."

"I heard that!" Kent blurts out, voice rough from sleep. "Seriously, one could be hiding in those pines."

Tim and I both laugh. I notice Kerry is still sound asleep in the corner bunk.

Kent asks, "Does someone have the coffee going?"

"Tim's got it going. By the time we get out of bed, it should be ready."

I unzip the sleeping bag, roll out of bed, put on a T-shirt and shorts, and step into my slippers. Good thing it's not too chilly in here. I take a peek at the thermometer as I walk into the kitchen—thirty-two degrees outside and sixty inside. Looks like some frost outside too. Nice. I prefer the weather to be on the colder side when deer hunting. Makes it feel more like camp—whatever that means. I look around the cabin. Sunlight is shining in through the windows. What a place. So much history. All you have to do is read the walls. Literally. For some reason, members and visitors, if so inclined, have peppered them with various scribblings of their experiences here.

11/15/1968—Opened camp 1pm. Stopped for late dinner in St. Ignace. Looking forward to a good camp this year. Bill

10/21/1964—Shot 3 grouse and 4 woodcock. Wet morning, with good tracking. Lady B came up a bit lame south of Huckleberry. Marie and I plan to hunt again later this afternoon if Lady is better. Doc

10/2/1976—Saw Tahquamenon Falls. Had dinner at the Sugar Shack in the Soo to celebrate Jigger's birthday. Fun time at TL. Mick, Maggie, Denny, Beth, Bill, Nancy, Del, Dianne

11/15/2005—First time at Trout Lake, deer hunting with Dad. This place is cool! CMB

Some of them are faded, and some look recent, but they are all over—even on doors and kitchen cabinets. Unfortunately, all on lead paint. Dave's wife brought up a lead test kit one time, and it "lit right up." She was worried about bringing their kids up here and exposing them to the lead. I guess we are OK as long as we don't eat the paint chips. Anyways, we don't want to scrape and repaint the place because of all of the writing on the walls. I look around at the old schoolhouse. No electricity. Copper plumbing running overhead to all the propane lights. The big, Duo-Therm fuel oil heater over by the sink, with the reflective doors to distribute the radiant heat. Gosh, that has to be sixty years old. I remember installing that thing with Dave about fifteen years ago. We smelled like fuel oil for the rest of the week! It works great as a stove too. We always have two tea kettles full of water on top of it, steaming away. Prior to the hot water system, that's how they made hot water for washing and doing the dishes. Heck, we even use it as a slow cooker now and then, by just putting the food on top of it and letting it cook. Works great for soups, stews, or reheating food. I laugh thinking about Kent's corned beef sitting up there for five days! And the doors work great for hanging gloves and hats out to dry.

Dave's and Tim's rooms occupy the west half of the kitchen and eating area. Behind me, through the doorway, is the front area where I am sleeping. We modified it a few years back after Uncle Billy passed away. At that time, there was a big twin bed by the door, an old battered bunk on the south wall, and Uncle Bill's bed on the west wall. We replaced Bill's bed with my son's old bunk bed. We tossed the battered bunk, and Dave and Uncle Denny each brought up bunks for the south wall to replace it. We can sleep seven up front, and Dave and Del can sleep two each in their rooms.

I look over at the percolator, bubbling away.

"Hey Tim, how long does the coffee have to perk?"

"Five minutes. Is it bubbling?"

"Yeah."

"I'll set my watch."

He must have crawled back into bed. I glance into the front room. Kent and Kerry are still in bed. Once the coffee is done, they'll no doubt come stumbling into the kitchen. I step up on the deck area, which is about six-feet deep and as wide as the cabin. We think that this is where the teacher's desk was located in the old schoolhouse. The sinks are up here now, along with the hot water system. On the east side is the main door out of the cabin, to the small porch where the coolers sit. I walk north through the narrow door between the sinks and into the newer addition. The propane, wall-mounted heater is on low, so I turn it up to the next level. Two more ceramic tiles light up. No need to get the lights, though. Looks like they left the windows opened a bit. Good. Even though the place has more cracks than a whorehouse, we like to keep a few windows just a smidge open to protect us from carbon monoxide. I look around at all of the "stuff" on the walls. Deer, partridge, and grouse mounts. A very large oil painting of a gorilla—I think Billy brought that up. Lots of framed photos of Uncle Tim and his buddies. We call them the "Grouse Boys." They come up every fall to bird hunt. More writing on the walls. Oh, and there she is! Ursula Reversible. That's what we call her. On the shelf in the corner. It's an early seventies picture puzzle of a naked Ursula Andress, which is reversible. Actually, it's pretty cool—to say the least. Billy framed it between two pieces of Plexiglas. We flip it front to back once in a while, just for the fun of it. Her hips look unusually large, though. Maybe it's the lighting in the photo, which is also really cool. One side of her body is lit and the other half is shaded. The nudity is somewhat respectable, if you ask me.

I continue further north and open the door to our "built-in" outhouse. The first section has a shower, and then you go through another set of doors to the toilet. As far as outhouses go, it's pretty nice. We keep the seat hanging directly above the Duo-Therm, so when you need to go, the seat is nice and warm. I look at the photo on the wall that Uncle Tim took of a license plate in Detroit. It's a vanity plate that says LIONHTR. The plate frame around it says, "50 Years of Crap Ball!" I chuckle out loud as I look at the picture. How appropriate. The Detroit Lions are so bad.

Finished, I go back into the main room and turn on the valve at the sink. The pump kicks on, the burner lights into action, and hot water is immediately running over my hands. I grab for the soap, wash, rinse, and twist the valve back into the off position. The water stops, but the pump runs for a few more seconds, repressurizing the system before it stops. I look at my watch. It's almost seven.

"Hey Dave, you up?"

"Yeah. Thinking about breakfast. What should we make?"

I hear Tim's watch go off, and at the same time, Kent comes in from the front room, stopping to peek into Tim's room.

"I'll get the coffee, Tim."

"Thanks!"

Kent turns off the gas on the burner and grabs some cups from the cupboard.

"You guys want sugar or cream?"

We all reply that black is just fine. Tim appears from his room, and Dave walks in from the other bedroom.

"I'll take cream and sugar, if you don't mind," says Kerry as he walks in from the front room, wearing a T-shirt and sweatpants.

I turn the radio on and search for a good station. I stop on one playing a Jackson Browne tune. Dave pushes the table out a bit and slides onto the bench seat. Tim moves in next to him on the other side of the bench. Kent, Kerry, and I pull out the other bench and have a seat. As Kent pours the coffee into the mugs, the steam swirls upward in rapidly evaporating trails. The table is littered with a newspaper, a couple bags of chips, a can of salted peanuts, and a bottle of Crown Royal. It's still wrapped in its familiar purple velvet sock, with a gold tie cord.

"How about some egg, sausage, and cheese breakfast sandwiches?" I finally reply to my brother.

Tim perks up. "That sounds good!"

Kerry lifts his cup of coffee up to his nose to take a deep whiff before taking a sip.

"Man, this smells great!"

"Sure does," Kent nods in agreement. "Nice and strong. Should get the plumbing working real good here in a few minutes."

Dave gets up, "Hey Mike, which cooler is yours? I'll get the sausage going."

"It's the white top, blue bottom one. Grab the eggs, English muffins, and cheese, too."

Tim hollers, "Dave, don't worry about the butter, we have a couple sticks in here."

Dave comes back in, pulls the cast iron, double-burner griddle down off the wall hook, sets it on the stove, and lights the front and back burners. I refresh my coffee, get up, and open the bag of English muffins. Lighting one of the burners, I place the old-school toaster rack over the burner and load it up with muffin halves.

"Tim, did you say you brought up some sugar beets?"

"Yeah, I did. About three big bags of them. We have more than enough for everyone."

"I'm going to run over to the South-Side after breakfast to get some feed. I'll make sure to get enough for all of us."

"You guys mind if I tag along? I want to get some beer," says Kerry.

"Not a problem," I tell Kerry. "After we get back, we can set up the blinds, come inside for lunch, and then head back out to do some bird hunting off Huckleberry. I hate to stir things up too much, but it's not like we see lots of deer up here anyways! We have a better chance of shooting birds than we do of shooting a deer."

Dave said, "I don't think we've shot a deer in the last two or even three years. Tim, didn't you shoot the last one?"

"Yeah. Shot it with Dad's gun. Gosh, I was so excited that day!"

"I remember that!" I say between sips of coffee. "Didn't you say that was the first deer you shot up here?"

"That's the truth. Can you believe it? All those years of hunting up here and never once shot a deer. Hard for me to believe, too. Maybe we'll get one this year. We should be due!"

I take the muffins off the burner rack, butter them, and put more on the toaster. Dave is putting the cooked sausage on a paper plate lined with some paper towels to soak up the grease.

"Hey, I'll do the eggs, so don't shut off the burners. Can you watch the muffins? And, if you don't mind, cut some cheese?"

"No problem. Where's the cheese? Oh, never mind, I see it."

I crack the eggs, drop them in the skillet, break the yolk, and add some salt and pepper. When the eggs are almost done, they're generously blanketed with cheese. In a few minutes, sausage, eggs, and muffins are on the table. No doubt a certain fast-food restaurant would be envious of our work! As we eat, plans are made for the day, and our expectations soar to shoot a buck tomorrow morning. After breakfast, we pile the silverware and dishes into the sink, and start getting dressed. The caffeine in the coffee does the trick, and we all take turns visiting the outhouse, heated toilet seat in hand. That's what I call first class, Trout Lake style!

CHAPTER 5

HUCKLEBERRY

The road trip to Mel's South-Side is uneventful. We load up two bags of apples, two bags of corn, and a bag of carrots. Kerry grabs a twelve-pack of Bud Light. Unfortunately, the cute gal at the counter acts as though she would rather be doing something else. I wouldn't exactly call her customer friendly. Her attitude is very unattractive. Unfortunate. Most of the people up here are super friendly and bend over backward to make you feel welcome. Maybe she didn't get the UP email on proper etiquette. Oh, well. We drive back to the cabin, and as we pull into the driveway, we notice that Tim's pickup is gone.

"Looks like Tim and Kent went out to prep their blinds," Kerry says.

We toss the bags of feed on the grass next to the porch and head inside to get our hunting gear on.

"Hey Kerry, can you carry my blind? Dave and I will carry the backpacks and feed."

"Sounds like a deal to me! Those straps cut into my shoulders."

"I know what you mean. I actually bought some strap pads for mine. They seem to help a bit. I told Dave I was going to get him some, but I keep forgetting!"

Dave hollers from the other room. "Yeah, thanks Mike. Christmas is a month away, hint."

I make a mental note of that one again. It should be an easy gift.

We load up the packs with a mix of sugar beets, carrots, apples, and corn. Each one must weigh about sixty pounds. Even with my strap pads, I can still feel the weight of the pack digging into both shoulders. My arms will be numb by the time I get to my blind. We grab our guns, walk across H-40, cross the tracks, and start walking south on Huckleberry. Two hundred yards later, we turn east, paralleling the edge of the woods on the right. A few minutes later, we enter into the woods and follow an old logging path. The path heads east for about a quarter mile and then turns south. We stop at the corner.

Dave looks at Kerry. "You should put a blind right here. There's a lane to the east where Kent saw a buck last year, and you also have a lane to the south."

Kerry props his shotgun in the crotch of a small tree and scans the area. I think he's trying to imagine being in the blind, to see if he has good shooting lanes.

"Yeah, this will work. We'll need to clear the lanes a bit, but I think this is pretty good!"

I remove my heavy pack, relieved that the weight is gone. Dave starts grabbing some small, inch-thick aspens and cuts them to about eight feet long. He will use them for the framework of the blind. Kerry and I start cutting low-hanging fir branches, to put over the framework. We create a four-sided, three-foot-high blind, with a small entry in the back. When we are done, Kerry sits in the blind and looks down each shooting lane.

"OK, we need to remove a couple of those branches right there," he says, pointing to the south.

Dave and I go down each shooting lane, hatchet in hand, following Kerry's pruning directions. In a matter of five minutes, we are done. Next, I grab my pack and spread some feed in each shooting lane, about thirty yards from the blind.

Finished, we pick up our packs and guns, and start walking south. We navigate over a small creek, maneuvering over railroad ties laid down by someone long ago. The creek flows west into a swamp, which feeds into a pond just to the east of Huckleberry. Across the creek now, and standing on the last tie, I look back toward Kerry's blind. That was the start of my Trout Lake journey, right there, fifteen years ago, when I shot my first buck. A seven point. *My gosh, fifteen years—where has the time gone?* I think to myself. After what seems like a few minutes, I take a deep breath, turn, and follow the guys through a small clearing between some aspens and then pop out onto a sandy area. This is where I dropped him. It was about a 150-yard shot. I remember looking up and there he was, just standing there, centered in the shooting path. If I hadn't looked up at just that moment, I probably wouldn't have seen him. Not many people have shot a buck on their first trip to Trout Lake, much less a seven point. Some have hunted for years and never shot one. Tim can testify to that.

"Man, has this place has grown over the last fifteen years. It was like an eight-foot-wide path when I shot that deer. You can't even see Kerry's blind from here now!"

Dave looks around and says to me, "You know, you could probably hunt this sandy area. There are deer tracks all over, and there is no way that you're going to be in Kerry's line of fire with all of these trees."

"Nah, I'll go back to my blind. This is a little too close for comfort."

Kerry nods in agreement, and we trudge on to the south, still following the logging trail. Taller maples line the left, and pine and aspen are on the right.

Suddenly, a thumping explosion rings through the forest.

"Grouse!" Someone hollers, followed by a couple of gunshots.

I look back at Kerry. "Did you get it?"

Kerry looks at me, then back into the woods. "Yeah, I think so."

Dave is already in the woods, and he picks up the bird.

"Looks like we have our appetizer tonight!"

We examine the grouse for a bit, and then Dave stuffs it into Kerry's game bag.

Dave says to Kerry, "I think you got it. I was too far away and just putting up some lead."

Kerry laughs. "They scare the shit out of you when they go up, and half the time you don't even have a shot through the trees."

Kerry loads a couple of shells into his Browning, replacing the two he shot. Dave breaks open his Citori, grabs the spent shell, and puts another 20-gauge shell into the breech.

"Doc hated those damn birds because they were so hard to hit. He would tell you to shoot them on the ground and stomp on their eggs!"

I could understand shooting them on the ground, but stomping on the eggs? I never did figure that one out, and any explanations given to me by the rest of the Trout Lake crew didn't make much sense. Must have been a "Doc" thing....

We get our bearings and continue on the logging trail. It makes a bend to the west, and within a hundred yards or so, we reach my hunting spot, tucked in between a couple of pines. Dave and I drop our packs, and Kerry hands me my portable blind. I pull it out of the pack and open it up. I doesn't take me very long to place it and put some stakes into the corners to keep it from blowing away. Taking a seat in the blind, I unzip the windows and peer down my shooting lanes to the south, east, and west. My back is to the woods. Kerry and Dave clear out some of the brush in each of the lanes, per my direction, and we are finished in about ten minutes.

Dave grabs his pack. "So where do you want the feed?"

"Drop some over by that small pine, and then some twenty yards down the south lane. Throw the rest over there to the west, right by that spot where it looks like something's been pawing at the ground."

Dave finishes putting down the feed, and I close up my blind. We pack our gear back into our backpacks and grab our guns.

"Hey, let's go out through the beaver dam," Dave suggests.

I'm hesitant and not too excited to go that way, for fear of getting wet or lost.

"You sure you know how to get through there?"

"Yeah, it shouldn't be too hard. After the clearing, we just keep heading west. You can see the tree line that surrounds the pond, and the beaver dam is on the south side of it. Should be pretty easy, especially during the day."

"Well, I guess if you know what you're doing...."

My brother, the human frickin' GPS, leads the way.

Our trek is straightforward and fairly uneventful, just as Dave predicted. It's pretty cool to see the beaver dam and the pond. But I can definitely see where someone could fall into the pond if they didn't know where they were going—especially in the dark. And speaking of dark, the water is black. Can't see the bottom at all. Past the pond, about fifty yards, we pop out of the woods onto Huckleberry, heading north toward the cabin. We pass Lanie's place, cross the tracks, and walk across H-40 to the cabin. Looks like Tim's nephew, Dave, has arrived. The sun is at high noon as shafts of light dance through the trees onto the forest floor.

CHAPTER 6

DL

Just as we get around the front of the cabin, Dave Lehman pops through the door, headed down to his SUV. He notices us, stops, and smiles. "Hey guys, good to see you!"

The three of us shake hands with DL, excited to see him.

"Kerry! Long time, no see! Glad you could make it up here this year. You going to stay longer than two days?"

My brother and I laugh, and Kerry just grins.

"Yeah, what the hell. I figured a few more days up here hunting with no shower and five guys isn't really that bad after all!"

We all get a good chuckle over that one. So true.

My brother reaches into DL's vehicle and grabs a sleeping bag. "Are you sleeping in your normal spot?"

"Yeah, just throw it on the bed. Thanks!"

"What can I carry in for you?" I say, looking around inside to see what might be good for the taking. Over there, a couple of gun cases.

Just like he read my mind, DL says, "Grab the gun cases, and throw them on the top bunk."

"You got it."

I take the guns inside and pass my brother going back out for more stuff. I hear DL tell one of them to put the cooler on the porch. Between the six of us, the small porch is getting crowded with coolers. I toss the gun cases on the top bunk, then head back out to see if there is more to bring in. I pop through the doorway, and DL is closing the rear hatch.

"You all set?"

"Yeah, my pack and stuff for the blind is all that's left. Man, the weather sure is beautiful! Nice and cool, with the sun shining. It doesn't look like it's going to get much above forty-five degrees this week. No rain in the forecast, either."

"Last year was too hot. Deer don't seem to move much when it's warm, but let's be honest, there aren't many deer up here anyway!"

"True."

I navigate my way through all the coolers and reach into mine for a beer.

"You need one?"

"Sure, what do you have?"

"Fat Tire, Stella, and Two Hearted."

"Two Hearted. Thanks!"

I yell, "Hey, anyone else need a beer?"

Kerry says yes, and my brother says no. I grab two Fat Tire's. We make our way through the narrow doorway, into the back room, to where Dave and Kerry are sitting. I hand Kerry a beer and grab a seat next to the propane heater.

DL takes a long swig of beer. "Damn, I hate getting up here late. What are you guys doing for the rest of the afternoon?"

"Well, we just set up Mike's and Kerry's blinds. Kerry is hunting at the first bend, where Mike shot that buck back in oh-one. Then we went back to where Mike's been hunting the last few years, dropped some feed, and got the hell out of there. We didn't want to make too much noise, but we did pop a grouse!"

DL's eyebrows arch upward. "Who shot it?"

Kerry laughs. "Well, that's to be debated. It was either Dave or me. I got a couple of shots off, and Dave got one off."

"I think you got it, Kerry. I didn't have much of a shot, and like I said, I was just putting up some lead. The more, the better."

"Where did you shoot it?" DL asks.

"A bit past the sandy area, to the south, in those aspens. Mike sees them frequently in there. Hey, we are going back out to get my blind ready. Do you need to get yours set up? We could hit it on the way to mine."

"That sounds great! Maybe we can nab a few more birds and make a meal out of it tonight? At least have some hors d'oeuvres. So, where's Uncle Tim and Kent?"

"I think they're out getting their blinds ready," I say. "Tim's hunting in the same spot off Huckleberry, south of you, and Kent was contemplating a new logging trail south off Huckleberry, about a half mile down after it bends to the east."

My brother asks DL how things have been going, and he fills us in on the past year. I take a swig of my beer and look at DL while he is talking to Dave. Damn, he looks more and more like his father, Del, every year. Even has a felt Stetson like his dad has. He looks good in it too. Some people can wear those hats, and they just look natural in them. I don't feel that way with my dad's hat. I always think people are looking at me like I'm some sort of dweeb. He has his dad's personality too. Easygoing. One of those guys that's really fun to talk with. He has some interesting hobbies, also. For example, he does home-brewed beer. A few years ago, he entered one of his brews into Bell's Brewery's Homebrew Competition and won! He called his entry Proud Mitten. As the winner, he got to work with Bell's Specialty Brewer and make Proud Mitten on their equipment. When it was ready, they tapped it at the brewery and at a Homebrewers' Conference in Grand Rapids. Pretty damn cool, to say the least. DL's quite the outdoorsman too—loves being in the woods and is pretty knowledgeable, like my brother. He has been coming up here since he was a kid, but went through a period in life where other things took priority and Trout Lake wasn't on the agenda. Funny thing is, now that he has been coming up here regularly, his dad has not. Quid pro quo. I look at my watch, finish my beer, and stand up.

"How bout we get loaded up and get going?"

DL gets out of his chair. "Sounds good to me. Give me a few minutes to change, and let's hit it!"

He disappears through the narrow doorway to get ready. Within ten minutes, the four of us are loaded up, guns in hand, feed packs on our back, walking down Huckleberry for the second time today.

CHAPTER 7

SPUR 447

The entry point to DL's blind is about a half mile down Huckleberry, just past the swamp, but on the west side of the road. We jump a small roadside ditch, climb the short bank, and head west down a wide trail. After about a hundred yards, the trail forks to the northwest and southwest. We take the southwest fork, and two minutes later, we are at the intersection of three different trails—one where we came from, one to the south, and another to the northwest. DL walks up to the remnants of his blind, which has not fared well since last fall. All that is left are three one-inch saplings that formed the frame. He steps over the saplings and looks down the trail to the south.

"Let's set it up same as before, with the main shooting lane to the south."

"Where to you want us to drop the feed?" I ask him as I set my gun against a small sapling.

"Fifty yards down each shooting lane."

Kerry grabs DL's pack and heads down one trail, while my brother and I hit the other two. We drop corn, apples, carrots, and sugar beets, and kick the pile around to spread it out. Darn fine meal for the critters, if you ask me! I start back toward the blind, and Dave is getting the framework set for some pine boughs. My brother grabs his machete and starts cutting branches. Kerry and I follow suit. We spend the next ten minutes cutting needle laden boughs and taking them to DL. He weaves them into the framework, creating his blind. Finishing up, he takes a seat in the structure. We spend the next five minutes trimming branches and ground cover in his shooting lanes. Task completed, we pack up and start walking to my brother's blind to repeat the drill. Leading the way, my brother heads down the south shooting lane for a hundred feet or so, then breaks off the trail to the southwest, in the general direction of his blind, about a quarter mile away. I don't see a trail but know we will cross a small creek in a minute, which appears in short fashion.

"You sure you know where you're going, Dave?"

"Yeah, that way," he says, with a quick wave of his hand.

Two years ago, I hunted in DL's spot, and Dave blazed a shortcut to his blind from there. It's a shorter distance than walking down Molly Gibson Road to the usual entry point. Using a compass and his general knowledge of the area, we started walking toward his blind. Dave used a machete to mark small trees on the path. Eventually, we zig-zagged our way to the main trail where his blind was situated. I walked that path a couple of times that season, and had to search more than once for the marks on the trees. I hate not knowing where I am in the woods, and even though all you have to do is walk north or east to hit a main road, there is no bigger fear than thinking you are lost in the woods up here. It's the main reason why I always carry a GPS and a spare set of batteries.

"Hey Dave, I don't see any marks on the trees. How the hell do you know where you're going?"

"It's not that far. The trail is just over there."

Sure enough, after a few minutes, we hit the trail, and to our left is the remnants of Dave's blind. In forty-five minutes, we have Dave's blind refreshed and the feed strategically scattered down his shooting lanes.

"Let's hunt the main trail back to Molly Gibson," Dave suggests.

"Great idea," says Kerry.

DL and I agree.

"Dave, why don't you stay on the path, and we can bust into the woods on both sides of you," I tell my brother.

"Sounds good!"

At this time of the year, the shooting isn't too bad in the woods—lots of pines and spruce saplings about ten- to fifteen-feet tall. Most of the leaves have dropped, so if a bird goes up, you'll get a good look. However, you still need to watch your step for fallen trees and dips in the earth. We call them "ankle breaks."

"Lots of coyote scat on the trail here—more than I've ever seen before," Dave announces from the main trail.

DL replies from the woods, "You sure it isn't bear shit?"

"Yeah, it's a coyote. Has some fur in it. Probably eating snowshoes."

All of a sudden, two quick gunshots ring out to the left of me, on the other side of Dave.

"Who shot?" Dave yells.

"Me," DL hollers back.

"Did you get it?"

"Yeah, I think so. I have the spot marked where it went down. Heading there right now."

"Kerry, where you at?" Dave hollers again.

I hear Kerry yell that he is heading over to help DL look for the bird. I stand there for a minute, just listening. Soon, I find myself looking to the east over a large swale, and into the woods where DL's blind is located, and then back to the north, where we are headed. There is so much land up here, and so little civilization.

"Hey, we got it!" Kerry yells.

Nice—that makes two for the day so far. We continue north, busting more brush, and put a few more birds up. We miss both of them. Eventually, we get to the edge of the woods and Molly Gibson Road. The railroad tracks run parallel to the road, and the cabin is a little less than a mile to the east. We choose to walk the tracks, which I prefer. Railroads are like taking a step back in time—used heavily in a different era, replaced by trucking now, along with other more economical means of transporting goods. Looking down, I see taconite pellets scattered between the ties and crushed gravel. They must have fallen through cracks in the ore cars. Pretty sure they pick them up somewhere in Wisconsin or Minnesota, and take them to the Soo. If I'm not mistaken, the *Edmund Fitzgerald* sank carrying a load of these pellets back in seventy-five.

Railroad spikes here and there. Loose and rotted ties. Some weird, crystallized, foamy stuff that is probably flux for welding the track sections together. They did that job about five years ago. Broken cutting discs here and there. Jeez, they could have picked this stuff up when they were done! Further up, we pass a marker on the side of the tracks. It's an old, weathered cedar post, with a rectangular sign at the top marked 447 in large black letters.

"Hey Dave, why is this here?" I ask, pointing at the sign.

"Pete told me that a spur used to be here. Spur 447. He said it branched off at this spot, curved to the north across H-40, and ran parallel to Wilwin Road, west of the cabin."

"I wonder what it was for."

"He said lumber. It was before his time."

Looking around, I don't see any indication that there was a spur going off to the north. No openings in the trees, no berms built up that would carry the track. It's just like it never existed, except for the sign. It sure must have been a long time ago—another place and time, long forgotten.

Five minutes later, we arrive at the cabin.

CHAPTER 8

DINNER

Standing next to the porch, DL and Kerry pull the birds out of their game vests and place them on one of the coolers. I grab one and fan the tail feathers to see if it's a male or female. I recall something about the males having a solid white band and the females having a broken white band. I show DL.

"This one looks like a male."

"Yeah, that's what I would say. Band isn't broken. I read somewhere that it isn't always true, but who knows for sure. All I know is they taste really good," DL chuckles.

"No doubt about that!"

The door to the cabin opens, and Tim and Kent appear, finally back from whatever they were doing.

My brother looks up and says, "When did you guys get back?"

Kent quickly replies, "Not too long ago—probably around three."

"Did you get your blinds all set?"

"Yeah, we did," says Tim. "It looks like that old guy that was hunting near me the past few years isn't there—at least it doesn't look like there has been any activity. Kent is way back on that trail, though. It took us a couple of trips to get his feed back in there. Man, was it muddy."

"It would have been worse if I didn't bring up that cart," Kent says, pointing toward Tim's pickup truck. Next to it on the ground is a muddy wheelbarrow-type cart with fat tires.

"Jeez, how far back are you?" I ask Kent.

"About a half mile, but there's deer signs all over the place!"

"Deer tracks don't mean anything. They are probably milling around in the middle of the night, not during the day."

"Oh, I think I will see some tomorrow. It's a great spot."

"Well, it would be nice to see you get one, Kent. You certainly have put in your time to get on the buck pole."

Tim laughs. "Yeah, he'd like to get on the buck pole alright!"

Everyone has a good chuckle at that one. Kent laughs too, appreciating Tim's quick humor.

Fortunately for Kent, Tim changes the subject.

"You guys given any thought to dinner tonight?"

Ah, yes. The laughing quickly subsides, eyes gloss over, and lips smack as the discussion turns to food. We might not "catch" many deer up here (as my lovely wife would say), but we sure do know how to put together a gourmet meal.

I set the bird down and say to Tim, "Well, I brought up those bacon-wrapped sirloin fillets. We can sauté some mushrooms and blanch some fresh green beans. Throw in some garlic bread, and I think that we have our first deer-camp dinner."

Everyone one agrees on the menu, and then attention turns back to the two grouse.

"How about we clean these two birds and cook the breasts with the mushrooms? Throw in an onion, some extra butter, and we'd have a nice side dish."

"I think that sounds great, Dave!" says Tim.

Tim and Kent head back inside, and Kerry and I follow. Dave and DL start to clean the birds. Kerry and I strip out of our hunting gear and get into some comfortable clothes. We finish by hanging our boots above the Duo-Therm heater, using a string and pulley contraption that my brother devised. It works great for drying wet clothes, too.

For the next hour or so, we all help prepare dinner like instruments in an orchestra, playing a symphony. No doubt our wives would be impressed by our culinary techniques. I wrap bacon around the fillets and get the grill going, while my brother flours the grouse breasts and sautés the onions and mushrooms. DL is preparing the green beans, while Kent is wrapping the garlic bread with aluminum foil, so we can put it on the grill. Of course, we all have drinks in our hands.

"I think that we should use the fine china for tonight's meal," Tim announces.

Everyone agrees, even though doing dishes would be more work than just throwing the paper plates into the trash. However, the hot water setup makes doing the dishes pretty darn easy. We finally sit down to eat, with the propane lights casting a yellowish glow over the room. The food smells great, and we all dig in. Talk centers around opening day tomorrow, and our excitement that one of us will shoot a buck. Eventually, we finish the meal. Every last bit of it. Kent announces that he'll handle the dishes, and my brother gives him a hand. I wander out to the back room with Kerry, DL, and Tim. We all sit down, full from the meal, and relax.

"Oh yeah, I almost forgot!

Tim suddenly gets up and heads into the other room. He returns with a couple of shoe boxes. "I found these at home over the summer. There are all kinds of neat photographs in here!" He dumps the contents of the shoe boxes onto the table, and we gather around to pick through the photos. Most of them are of the Lehman family, but some are of my grandfather, Doc, and my grandma, Marie. We even find a letter that Doc wrote to Doyle, who was in the army at the time. Doyle is Mott's son, Tim's and Del's father, and DL's grandfather. Doc was between Mott and Doyle in age, and he hung out with both of them. Just like the three musketeers. Soon, Dave and Kent finish the dishes and wander in to check out the photos. We all have a blast looking at them. Quite a few are from Trout Lake. It's fun to imagine what it was like back then. My only memory of Trout Lake with my grandparents was when I was about four years old, getting a bath with my brother in this big galvanized tub on the kitchen table.

We spend the next couple hours poking through the photos, having a few drinks, and talking about the history of the cabin. At about eleven, the group starts to break up and get ready for bed. Tim gets the coffee prepped, and the rest of us lay out our hunting clothes and brush our teeth. The usual routine. Finally, at about eleven-thirty, all of us are in bed, except for my brother, who is outside. I hear him come back in, shut the door, and put the threaded bolt through the hasp lock on the door. A couple of propane lights are still flickering, casting shadows. A few seconds later, they get shut off. As my eyes adjust to the darkness, dancing orange flames become visible through the Duo-Therm sight glass. The light reflects softly off the walls of the kitchen. It's mesmerizing.

"Hey Dave, did you throttle down the heater?" I ask quietly.

"Yeah, I did. We should be good."

"OK, good night."

"Yeah, good night, Mike."

I fluff the pillow and get comfortable. I gaze out the window to the east, toward town. I wonder if the train will be coming from that direction tonight. I wonder if I will wake up when it rolls through. I also wonder how many times I will need to get up to take a leak! My mind stays active with plenty of random thoughts and musings. I allow myself a small chuckle as I drift off to sleep, happy and content to be back up in the cabin, where life is simpler, the land is vast, and time floats by like the wind through the trees. As I drift off to sleep, a train's horn faintly sounds off in the distance.

CHAPTER 9

OPENING DAY

Beep-beep…beep-beep…beep-beep! I roll over, grab my phone, and tap the screen. The beeping stops. The light from the screen illuminates my face, and the sudden brightness makes me squint. Finally, my eyes adjust. Six fifteen. OK, if I lay in bed a bit more, someone else will get up and get the coffee going. I look out the window and see a set of headlights approaching. As the lights get closer, the sound of large, deeply treaded tires break through the morning silence. It's a school bus—the one that Sonja drives. She is on her way to pick up the first riders. These kids will sit on the bus for about two hours, until they get to the school in Rudyard. Talk about a long bus ride! The whine of the tires lulls as the bus makes a right-hand turn onto Wilwin Road. Honk! Sonja hits the horn for us. We always joke with her to blare the horn when she drives by, to make sure we are up. Not wanting to disappoint her, I get out of bed, throw some clothes on, and head for the kitchen. After lighting a couple of lamps, I get the burner going under the coffee pot. The hissing sound of the lamps cuts through the silence of the cabin. As I unlock the front door and step outside to relieve myself, the cold air hits me and I shiver. Damn, it's freezing out here! The morning is still dark, and the sky is clear. Heading back inside, I see Kent sitting at the kitchen table. Kerry is digging around for something on the top bunk, under the soft light of the propane lamp. No sign of DL, Tim, or my brother.

"Good morning, Kent."

"Good morning to you too. How did you sleep?"

"Not too bad, actually. Did a train go by last night?"

"Yeah, about three in the morning. Long one too. You didn't hear it?"

"No, I didn't. I slept right through the night."

Kerry comes in from the front room, says good morning, and heads directly outside. DL appears next and grabs a seat next to Kent. Soon after, my brother enters the room.

"Hey guys, good morning."

We all mutter "Good morning" in unison, still groggy with sleep. Dave reaches down and gives the knob on the Duo-Therm carburetor a slight counterclockwise twist to kick up the heat and opens the side doors wide. In a few minutes, the flames will be dancing furiously behind the sight glass, pouring forth heat into the room. He walks over to the front window and takes a peek at the thermostat.

"Looks pretty cold outside—near thirty. Might be a bit crunchy walking into the woods this morning, with some frost."

Kerry comes back inside and similarly announces, "We have frost on the ground, fellers. It might be a bit noisy walking in woods this mornin'."

"I was just looking at the temp outside and thought the same thing," Dave chuckles as he grabs a seat at the table.

Tim finally makes his appearance in long johns, a T-shirt, and those funny-looking slippers. I'll have to remember to look them up on the internet when I get back home, to see what brand they are. He wishes everyone a good morning and eyes the coffee pot over on the gas burner.

"Who got the coffee going?"

"I did. Hopefully, the grounds are in there, because I didn't look."

"Yeah, they are. I got it ready last night, before bed. I made it nice and strong to help get things moving, if you know what I mean. There's nothing worse than having to find a place to go as soon as you get to your blind!"

Kent notices that the coffee is starting to perk.

"Set the clock. Five minutes!"

"So, are you guys hungry?" my brother asks. "I can cook up some bacon, eggs, and toast."

All nod in agreement, thankful that Dave is offering to cook. We typically stay out in the woods longer on opening day, and a big breakfast would be nice. Dave heads out to the porch to grab the food, while the rest of us disperse to start getting ready. Soon after, Tim announces that the coffee is ready, and the group quickly reassembles at the dinner table to have a cup of java and watch Dave cook. Well, everyone except Kent, who walks over to the Duo-Therm and removes the toilet seat from the hook. We know where he is heading, envious that he will have one less thing to deal with while in the woods.

Tim chuckles and says, "Jeez Kent, you just sniffed that coffee and now you're off to the races!"

"I'll make sure to get things all warmed up for you guys! First is always best in this situation," Kent says with a shrug, as he turns through the doorway, toilet seat in hand.

I look over to Dave. "Hey, you need some help?"

"Sure. Butter the toast."

The smell of bacon and eggs is heavy in the air. DL gets some paper plates, napkins, and silverware, and Tim goes outside to grab the orange juice. The table is prepped, and we sit down to eat. Kent makes it just in time, no doubt lured by the smell of bacon and eggs wafting through the cabin.

"So Kerry, do you want to head out together?"

"Yeah, that sounds good. What time do you want to leave?"

"I'm thinking like seven fifteen or seven thirty. Sunrise is before eight, and we should be able to be in our blinds by then. That shouldn't be too late. I don't think any of us has shot a deer before nine anyways."

Heads nod in agreement with that statement as we scarf down our breakfast. Within five minutes, all that remains of the meal are a couple pieces of toast laying on a greasy piece of paper towel that once held the bacon. Plates go into the trash, and for the next half hour, we get dressed, load up our gear, and take turns heading to the outhouse, toilet seat in hand.

"Hey Kerry, you about ready?"

"Almost, just give me a few more minutes."

Tim and Kent left about fifteen minutes ago, and my brother and DL are just walking out the door.

"Hey, good luck and be safe!" I call to both of them.

"Same to you," DL replies.

"I'll be listening for your gunshots this morning! Get that big buck," my brother says with an optimistic voice.

Kerry walks in from the front room fully dressed, with his rifle. I shut off the kitchen lamps, turn down the Duo-Therm heater, and grab my gun. We both walk out, and I shut the door behind us, lock the hasp, and hang the key in the hiding spot. Standard procedure. We cross H-40 and start down Huckleberry. As we cross the tracks, I look each way to see if anything is coming. Nothing. There is a train that normally comes through in the morning. In fact, a few years back, while I was walking to my blind, a long train was going through. You wouldn't think you could hear the train while in the woods, but you can. Actually, it's very clear. You can even hear the wheels going click-clack on the track. Anyways, I got to my blind and sat down just as the train was nearing town, the noise subsiding. As I got comfortable, I heard a twig snap directly behind me. Surrounded by small pines, I couldn't see if anything was on the other side of the trees and didn't think much of it. As I sat there, I kept hearing this weird noise—like something was breathing. Finally, after about five minutes, I stood up and looked around, and I'll be damned if a buck didn't take off! I had no shot—all I saw was his butt and tail as he ran in a straight line away from me. It looked like a five or six point, too. The moral of the story is to be prepared. He didn't hear me getting settled into my blind because of the train noise. In fact, he must have walked right up behind me!

"Let's go in here," I suggest to Kerry, pointing at a gap through the pines along the road.

We walk east through the field following the edge of the woods and quietly load our guns. Five minutes later, we enter the woods single file, with Kerry behind me. Communication ceases as we walk carefully, leaves crunching under our boots from the frost. Soon we reach Kerry's blind, and I wish him good luck. I head south, across the small stream and through the sandy area. Five minutes later, I arrive at my blind. Unfortunately, the bait looks undisturbed, which means no deer activity. Go figure. I unzip the blind's door, get in, and unzip the front and side windows. Damn, these zippers are noisy! I close up the entry door and settle down into my seat, making some minor adjustments so that I can get my gun up comfortably to a shooting position. Finally, I set my rifle down against the corner of the blind, pull my coat sleeve back, and glance at my watch. Seven fifty. Let the hunt begin!

CHAPTER 10

THE HUNT

I take a deep breath and look around. My breath vaporizes in the cold morning air, drifting to the north, behind me. That's good. I'm upwind from my shooting lanes. I adjust my seat and look around. It's quiet now, but that will soon change. After the shock of me entering the woods fades, the animals will start moving again. The sun is coming up, shining through the trees. Flecks of frozen water droplets pepper the blind. I stare at the droplets and watch them liquefy from the sun's rays. A titmouse lands in the sapling next to me and chirps. A raven flies overhead, its low, croaking sound echoing throughout the woods. Its wings make a swooshing noise as it passes overhead. The sounds of nature are so amazing when you take the time to listen and, boy, will I have some time.

In the next half hour, more birds appear, including a grouse. The perfectly camouflaged bird moves slowly, taking a few steps, stopping, then taking more steps. The head turns to look in one direction and then the other. Its movement appears random, with no obvious pattern. Maybe this technique protects them from predators. If you aren't looking in the right spot, you wouldn't even notice that the bird is there. The grouse is headed for the corn spread on the ground.

Suddenly, leaves crunch to my left. Once, then twice. I slowly turn my head, looking to pinpoint the source of the movement. Another crunch, and then another. Is it a deer? I can't get a good look, because the sound seems to be coming from within heavy cover. Again, a crunch, then another two. I sit motionless, looking for movement. I can feel my heart beating. Suddenly, the chatter of a red squirrel breaks the silence of the morning, right where I'm looking. It's a damn squirrel! I hate those little shits. And sure enough, right on cue, the little rascal hops out from the edge of the woods and darts across the shooting lane. He perches himself on top of a stump and starts to bark. I grab my gun and aim it at the rusty-colored noisemaker. Watching him through the four-power scope, his tail twitches with every bark. It is ridiculous how many times I have mistaken squirrel noise for a deer. You think I would learn a lesson after a few of these episodes, but nope—no such luck. I put the gun back down and sit back in the chair.

For the next fifteen minutes, I scan the shooting lanes, looking for movement. I swear that deer can appear right out of thin air. You can be looking down one lane, then turn your head the other way, and a deer will be standing there, looking at you. It's a bit disturbing. At least the frost will help me hear one coming.

Suddenly, from the west, I hear the train's horn—two long bursts and a short one. Must be going through Rexton. It should be here in about ten minutes. A few minutes later, the hum of the big diesels can be heard, getting louder as the train approaches. Again the horn lets out two long bursts and one short one as the train approaches Huckleberry. It roars through the crossing, headed toward town. Eventually, the humming and clacking subside into the morning air, broken only by more horn blasts as the train reaches Trout Lake.

I adjust in my seat, looking at my vintage, wool, red-and-black checked pants and jacket. Timber King brand, I think. My dad purchased it sometime in the early seventies, at a hardware store in downtown Clare. I should really buy a new one, but out of nostalgia and limited use, I continue to wear it. The pants fit fine, except one leg cuff is so tight that I can barely get my foot through it. And the jacket is so tight under my arms that I can barely get the gun up to shoot. But it's warm, and wool is great for wet weather. Maybe I'll look for a new one this spring, when they go on sale.

My eyes drift from the hunting suit to my rifle. Again, my dad's. It's a Winchester Model 100, .308 caliber. I run my fingers over the basket-weave imprint on the fore grip and stock. It probably counts as my rifle now, since I shot my first buck with it back in eighty-six and have shot two more since then. Dad's been using his father's .38 Remington pump. My thoughts drift to him—too bad the old boy isn't up here hunting with us. I can't blame him, though. He has already done his fair share of hunting up here. And I'm sure retirement in Florida for seven months of the year isn't too bad of an alternative. Now that I think of it, I've never been up here with him to deer hunt. He pretty much came up every year when I was young. But I was in sports, so I couldn't take the time off. Then, college happens, and then you get married, and then you have kids. Priorities change. When I was finally ready to start coming up, I didn't make the trip because of work. Instead I chose to cover for guys that worked for me, so they could go. Seemed like the right thing to do, since it was a yearly tradition for them. Then, about fifteen years ago, my brother suggested that I come up for deer camp. I had just lost my job in September, right after the World Trade Center bombing, and he thought the trip would be good for me. It was, and I haven't missed an opening day since.

I wonder what it was like up here with Doc and his buddies. I think my dad was up here then. Were they wild, drinking it up, playing cards, or did they just use the trip to unwind from the stresses of the real world? We sure as hell don't shoot many deer up here, so they must have found something else they liked about Trout Lake.

And what was Doc like? Tim remembers quite a bit, because he came up frequently with Del, his dad, Doc, and some of the other crew. He says that Uncle Bill was a lot like Doc. I can't personally verify that statement, but others have said the same. He said that Doc would pre-mix martinis in a jug and bring it to deer camp. My dad claims that's not true, and I always thought Doc preferred liqueur-type drinks, like Amaretto and Cointreau. I can't picture him drinking martinis. Tim also said that Doc did most of the cooking. He would pin the menu for the week on the hutch—breakfast, lunch, and dinner. Now that I can picture. Bill also liked to cook when he was with us. Gosh, he would use so much butter, and he'd get just about every pan dirty in the process. I should know, because I've done the dishes after Uncle Bill cooked! All that butter is probably why the food tasted so good. Boy, he sure could make some awesome sautéed apples! Yeah, I'm pretty sure that Doc liked food. Heck, who doesn't? We don't come up here just to hunt. We really come up here for friendship and great meals. I sink lower in the chair and pull my collar up around the back of my neck. The sun is higher now, and I can feel its warmth on my face. I extend my legs out a bit. Yeah, there we go. That feels better....

CHAPTER 11

LE PREMIER SAUT

Crack! My eyes snap wide open and dart toward the sudden noise, right in front of me. What was that? My eyes adjust to the light, and I see a deer looking right at me, about twenty-five yards away. The rack is huge! OK, be calm. It's a monster UP buck! My heart starts to pound as the adrenaline rushes through my body. I must have startled him when I woke up. What the hell—did I fall asleep? Shit, I need to grab the gun! Slowly, without taking my eyes off him, I reach for my rifle, grab it, and slowly pull it toward me, careful not to let the strap buckles clank on the metal barrel and receiver. Slow. Be careful. The buck turns his massive head to look behind him. He lowers his tail and wags it side to side a few times. He looks back in my direction and then straight ahead. Another couple wags of the tail. OK, he doesn't know that I'm here. I bring the gun up and, at the same time, push in the safety, being careful to avoid that metallic "snap." The deer takes a few steps forward, stops, and looks at me again. I look through the scope and put the crosshairs right behind and below the front shoulder. I exhale slowly, preparing to pull the trigger. Suddenly, I hesitate as a warning goes off in my brain. Something's not right. I lower the gun and stare at the trees.

"What the hell?" I say aloud.

The buck hears me and bolts away in long, graceful leaps, its tail high like a flag, with white underfur waving good-bye to me. The adrenaline surge from seeing the deer suddenly turns to panic as I scan the woods around me. Gone are my shooting lanes and familiar looking trees. I am now looking at a mature forest of hardwood, all around me. Standing up, I move my chair out of the way and unzip the door of the blind. I step out and scan the area, trying to figure out what's going on. Am I dreaming? Where the heck am I? I fumble for my compass. The blind still seems to be pointing in the same direction, but the sun is more to the west. Overcome by panic, I go down on one knee. Staying there for a few minutes, I eventually start to feel better. Logical thoughts start to take over. Assess the situation. Take everything in. Try to understand why everything looks so *different*. I have to do something.

"OK," I say out loud while maneuvering my compass. "That would appear to be east."

I glance up, looking east, but don't see the old logging trail. Where am I? I let out a nervous chuckle, and then, an idea hits. My phone! I reach into the front pocket of my coat, only to find no phone. Damn, I must have left it back at the cabin. Wait, GPS! I look down on my chest to see nothing hanging from my neck. I must have left them both back at the cabin. I finally stand up and look around again. The sun is higher in the sky and more toward the west. Weird. A quick pull on my left coat sleeve reveals that the time is two o'clock, November 15th. Gosh, last I remember, it was morning. I somehow lost a big chunk of time. Doubt and panic start to creep back in.

"Just do something, you jackass!" I holler out loud.

Just then, to the north, I hear the mechanical noise of a vehicle. Something is different about the sound, though. It doesn't sound...*normal*. But it's definitely an automobile. That's it! Follow the compass north, and I should eventually get to a road. I walk over to the blind and grab my gun. I can leave the rest here. Settling the compass, I look for a landmark to the north and start walking through the woods. Yeah, it's certainly different. This should be full of small pines and new-growth aspen. Instead, it's all large oaks and maples, with hardly any undergrowth.

"Unbelievable," I say aloud.

Within five minutes, I reach a small stream. I look around, but don't see a sandy area or any railroad ties bridging the creek. I hear another automobile in the direction that I'm walking. A good sign. Sighting north with the compass again, I pick another landmark, wade through the water, and continue onward. Soon, the woods starts to thin and a field comes into view, bordered by a road. As I reach the field, a truck appears on the road, driving at a moderate pace. Boy, that's one oldie of a truck. It looks like Fred Sanford's truck on that TV show back in the seventies—with a rounded front end, big chrome bumper, and step-side bed. The truck passes by an old, yellowish schoolhouse that suddenly captures my attention. That's so weird. It looks like our cabin but, yet, different. Dumbfounded,

I just stare at it for what seems like an eternity. It's sitting all alone on a plot of land, with no trees around it, and out front is a shed. About a half mile to the right is another small, white house. That looks like Pete's uncle Leo's place. So where is Pete's and Rod's house? Both should be between Leo's house and that old schoolhouse. There is another white house across the street from the old schoolhouse. I wonder if that's Lanie's place? It kind of looks like it, but something looks different there, too. I transfer the gun to my left hand and snug the stock under my armpit. I remove my right-hand glove and pinch my neck as hard as I can.

"Ouch!" I blurt out.

So much for that stupid idea. I guess it means I'm not dreaming. I let out a nervous laugh. More curious now than panicked, I walk west, following the tree line. I keep looking at the schoolhouse, trying to process the difference between what I see and what I think I should be seeing. As I walk, a black shape starts to appear between the schoolhouse and the shed. Fifty yards further, the shape becomes a car. Gosh, that looks old too. Suddenly, two long and one short horn blast can be heard, carrying through the air. Faint, but recognizable. A train! A few minutes later, a road becomes visible straight ahead. A low, rumbling and humming can now be heard. As I continue to walk, it grows louder, gaining strength. Finally, I step though some brush, jump across a small roadside ditch, and land on a gravel road. Standing in the middle of the road, I look to the south. The road continues about a quarter mile and rises up to a hump. The train is much louder now. Looking back north, I can see the tracks a couple hundred yards away and start walking toward them. The white house on the right comes into full view, but the schoolhouse is blocked by roadside brush.

The locomotive's horn pierces the air, announcing the impending arrival at the crossing. Two long blasts and one short. With a thundering roar, a yellow and maroon Soo Line, EMD F7A locomotive roars through the crossing, its split-windshield angled back atop a rounded, aircraft-like nose. Two headlights, one high and one low, shine bright. The engineer waves at me from an open side window in the cab. I numbly wave back. I notice the number 213B on the nose of the locomotive. Jaw agape, I watch as the boxcars cross the road, one by one. Having some knowledge of the Soo Line locomotives, I know that they have not operated one of these classic F7 series since the late sixties. Where the hell did this one come from?

Glancing back at Lanie's house, or what I *think* is Lanie's house, I notice a large canvas tent pitched in the yard and a light blue, four-door sedan parked on the grass. That's an old one too! What's with all of the old cars, trucks, and trains? I squint and notice *Biscayne* on the rear quarter panel. Isn't that a Chevy? Fifties or sixties? Gosh, look at that trunk. It's like a big v-wing. Hanging on a pole, next to the tent, is a buck with a nice rack. The trees around the house are so small! Where are all the big trees that should be there? And where is the pole barn, where Pete keeps his muscle cars? Instead, there's just a regular barn! A couple of old-looking John Deere tractors are parked in the grass. One looks like a model B, with the cambered, twin steer tires. Why is this stuff here?

Baffled, I look back toward the schoolhouse, catching flashes of it between the boxcars as they roll through the crossing. I walk closer to the track and get down on one knee to get a better view under the boxcars. Yeah, it kind of looks like our cabin, but the front of it is different, and the back end is missing something too. And the trees. Where the hell are the large pines in the backyard? It's just sitting in the middle of flat, barren ground. And what's with the yellowish color? It should be brown-colored, like aged cedar siding that we never maintained. The train horn blasts in the distance. Just as the short horn sounds, the caboose glides through the crossing, and the schoolhouse suddenly comes into full view. Standing up, I watch the flashing, red light, mounted to the coupler of the caboose as it passes by.

"There goes Oscar!"

Startled, I quickly turn around to face a slightly younger man with a salt-and-pepper goatee. He is holding a gun and wearing a dark brown Stetson, with a zebra-print ribbon. I open my mouth to ask him what he just said, but instead, I blurt out, "Grandpa?"

CHAPTER 12

DOC

The man with the Stetson laughs, and says, "Grandpa? You're as old as me!"

I just stand there, dumbfounded, staring at the man. What the hell is going on? What is he doing here? A wave of panic hits me like a hammer, and my vision starts to darken. Shit! I bend over, then go down on one knee. Struggling not to panic more, I take some deep breaths, but it's too late. The world is fading away. In a distant voice, I hear the man with the Stetson speaking to me.

"Hey, are you alright? You don't look so…"

I have only passed out twice in my life. The first time, I was giving blood and hadn't eaten for about eighteen hours. I watched as the nurse stuck the needle into my arm, and as my blood filled the vial, my vision started to darken. I looked at the nurse and told her as calmly as I could that I was about to pass out. And I did. Slumped right over in my chair. The other time was after I had a couple of margaritas, and unfortunately, I later discovered that I was allergic to tequila or, more specifically, the agave root. Anyways, waking up after fainting is pretty weird. It's even harder to describe. You first feel like you are in la-la land, and then you start to see faint images and hear muffled noises. Things keep getting clearer and clearer, and eventually the fog lifts. Finally, the cold sweats arrive for the encore.

"…Just relax. There you go, just relax."

Blue and white…muddled noise…a dark blob… Clearer now, focus coming back. I see the sky and clouds, and hear a train horn in the distance. Two long blasts and one short. The dark blob becomes the man with the Stetson. He is looking down at me. Is this a dream? Groggy and confused, I start to sit up.

"Woah there, buddy…stay there for a minute. You passed out. Looked like you saw a ghost before you went down. May I ask if you have any health issues? Are you on any medications?"

The cool air feels good on my face as the sweat breaks out.

"No, no health issues. No meds. Just kind of got a little anxious, I guess. Then it snowballed."

"Anxious about what?"

"Not sure, I guess," I lie. "I think that you kind of startled me…. Actually, you scared the shit out of me. I didn't know you were behind me."

I finally sit up, with the help of the man giving me a hand. I wipe the sweat off my face. My chest and back are now damp with sweat, and I'm starting to feel chilled.

"Sorry about that—I didn't mean to startle you. I came out of the woods and saw you up ahead of me. You must not have heard me because of the train noise. Eventually, I was standing right behind you, wondering why you were on your knees and looking under the train."

I glance at the yellowish tainted schoolhouse. "I was trying to get a better look at that schoolhouse over there."

He looks puzzled. "And why is that?"

I laugh nervously and say, "I'm not sure."

A look of concern washes over his face, probably because I'm not making much sense.

"It looks like your color is coming back. Do you want to try to get up?" He stands up and holds out his hand.

"Yeah, thanks."

"No problem. Name's Francis Boudreaux, but you can just call me Doc."

No shit, I think to myself as I shake his hand.

"Nice to meet you Doc, I'm…uh, Mike."

"Well, nice to meet you, Mike."

He brushes some dirt off my coat, then picks up my gun. He examines it like someone familiar with firearms.

"Nice gun. Hmm. Winchester?" Doc asks as he runs his fingers across the basket-weave checkering.

"Yeah, Model 100, .308 caliber."

"I didn't know that Winchester made a Model 100. Is it new?"

"No, been hunting with it for years. It was my dad's gun, but I sort of inherited it after shooting a couple more deer with it than he did."

I chuckle. Doc smiles and hands me the gun.

"Why don't we go check out that old schoolhouse, and I can make sure you're OK."

"Huh?"

"That's my place you're looking at. And I just happen to be a doctor, so I want to make sure you're doing alright after that little faint spell."

I can't help but smile. "Must be my lucky day."

Doc laughs. "I guess you're right."

We cross the tracks, and as we approach the main road, I look at the road sign. Huckleberry. Well, I'll be damned—what a coincidence. We cross the road and walk around the front of the schoolhouse. I hesitate and try to make sense of what I'm seeing. The schoolhouse looks exactly like the old photos I've seen. It's the same main building, with the front addition that my dad and Tom Banks tore off back in the early seventies. (They used a pickup and a chain!) And there is the back addition, roof sagging like an old horse's back. I wonder if the toilet is in the back corner. I look up at the soffit and then it hits me: The soffits on our cabin have a yellowish tint to them! Could this be the same schoolhouse?

"Hey Mike, the door's over here," Doc says as he turns the corner of the cabin.

I glance at the shed out front. The darn thing looks so good—no scrub brush around it, it's not leaning, and the roof is intact. Still staring at the shed, I almost run into a black car parked next to the cabin. I can tell by the emblem on the hood that it's a Cadillac. An older one, like fifties or sixties, but man, is it in great shape! No rust. Kind of like that Chevy across the street. This one is a two-door hardtop, with a sloping rear window—very elegant. Tall fins sit atop both rear fenders, each with two red, bullet-shaped taillights mounted right in the middle of the fins, pointed rearward.

"Whoa! I guess I better watch where I'm going! Nice car, by the way. Cadillac?"

"Yeah, fifty-nine Seville."

"Still looks good after all these years."

Doc stops on the steps and turns around. He has a confused look on his face.

"What do you mean, after all these years? It's practically new. Bought it last year."

"Uh…yeah, what the heck am I saying? Must still be a bit foggy."

I let out a weak laugh, and Doc looks at me with slight concern. Then he turns around and puts a key into the padlock, opens the door, and steps inside. I take another look at the shed and the Cadillac, shaking my head and trying to make sense of the situation. I'm so confused. Finally, I take a deep breath, climb two steps, and walk through the doorway. It takes a couple of seconds for my eyes to adjust from the brightness outside, and then the inside of the old schoolhouse becomes visible. There has to be some explanation for this. It would appear that I've somehow stepped back in time and just met my grandfather, who died forty years ago.

CHAPTER 13

THE CABIN

It is all so surreal. The inside of the cabin looks the same yet different—more bare. Over the years, the old cabin has become a final resting place for the members' "stuff." This stuff should have been thrown out back home instead of being brought up here. I guess you could call it man-cave decor, deer-camp antiques, or pieces of art thought to be meant for a place like this. But the "stuff" gets to be overwhelming. Trout Lake tchotchke—that's what I call it. Looking around, this schoolhouse looks clean, almost sterile. I'm not sure I like it this way. Seems less welcoming, cold. Doc opens a box of matches, finds one, and lights two propane lamps over the dinner table. The lights hiss-pop to life, and the room brightens slowly.

"This place isn't too bad for an old schoolhouse," I manage to blurt out, in a weak attempt to break the silence. I remind myself to act natural, steadying each breath.

"Yeah, it's not fancy, but we really enjoy it. Pretty low maintenance, if you know what I mean."

Doc lights two more lamps over the stove. Hiss-pop!

By the light of the lamps, I can see the room much more clearly. Different stove. Same cabinet in the corner. Same dinner table. And what do you know—a Duo-Therm heater! Not the same as the one Dave and I installed, but maybe it's the one we replaced. How can this be? Turning around, I see the same white porcelain sink by the front door. No on-demand hot water system, though. Looks like the fuel oil tank for the Duo-Therm is inside. It must stink like hell in here if they spill any of that heavy fuel oil. And there it is: a toilet seat hanging on a nail right above the heater! Some things never change.

"Well, it looks like you have a warm seat if you need to use the bathroom!"

"Hey, this is a first-class operation around here! The outhouse is just beyond that door, right there."

Doc points over my shoulder to the narrow door next to the sink. I walk over to the door, open it, and take a look. Sure enough, the toilet is in the back corner. A few magazines and a couple rolls of toilet paper lay on a makeshift table next to it. Wood planks pave the way to the toilet, just like in the old black-and-white photos. I suddenly recall one of Doyle on the toilet, hunting pants around his ankles, reading a newspaper. I think he was wearing an Elmer Fudd hat—you know, with the furry ear flaps.

"It's not too bad of a setup, as long as you don't mind the mice running across your feet once and a while."

"Are you serious? Mice?"

Doc just grins. I'm not sure if he's telling the truth. Uncle Bill would say the same thing, though. I shut the door and take a few steps forward to where the floor drops down about a foot.

"So why is the floor higher up here?" I ask, already knowing the answer.

"We think that the teacher sat up there and the students were down here."

"Yeah, that would make sense. How old is this place?"

"Built at the turn of the century. It was originally across the street. They moved it sometime in the thirties, I think. Four of us bought the place in forty-eight. This is the kitchen and dining area. That's the front room over there."

Doc turns and walks through another doorway. I follow after him, carefully scanning the room. It looks different from what I'm familiar with. No bunk beds—rather, three small twin beds and one full bed. No junk hanging on the walls. Next to the beds are some pots painted with floral designs. They look familiar!

"What are the pots for?" I say, pointing to one of them.

"Well, we pee in them at night instead of getting out of bed. Who wants to get out of a warm bed and go into a cold outhouse?"

We both laugh. I think those same pots now hang on the wall of our cabin for decoration. Doc walks through another set of doors, into the front-most room. This one does not look familiar to me. My thoughts begin to race as the realization dawns: Was this the room that Dad helped tear off all those years ago? But how can this be?

"We call this the Catholic room, because the floor is full of holes. Holy. Get it?"

We both laugh.

Doc kicks at a piece of plywood laying on the floor, which slides a few feet, revealing a big hole.

"We don't really have much use for this room, but we haven't figured out what to do with it. This was a store before we bought it, and we are pretty sure that this was the storefront."

"Well, maybe you could just tear it down?"

"Hey, that's not a bad idea! Anyways, that's the grand tour. Why don't we go back in there so you can have a seat and I can take a look at you?"

"Uh, OK, I guess."

Doc walks past me and grabs a black bag sitting on the bed. As I pass through the doorway, I notice a calendar hanging on the door. What a coincidence—we always hang a calendar in that exact spot. I look closer at the calendar. It's from Lehman Hardware. Wait…Lehman Hardware? That's been closed for years! I pull the calendar off the nail. The cover is a painting of a grouse, flushing from cover with an English setter on point. It's flipped to November 1960. 1960?! I guess that explains a few things…kind of. I feel dizzy again, steadying myself by placing my hand against the wall.

Doc motions at the kitchen table. "Why don't you take off your jacket and sweater, and have a seat? Just throw your stuff right on the table."

I peel off my layers, toss them on the table, and have a seat on the bench. Doc opens up the black bag, pulls out a stethoscope and a blood pressure cuff, and sets them on the table. Then he pulls out a small black object that looks like a flashlight.

"OK, look straight at me, if you don't mind."

He looks into each of my eyes with the flashlight, moving the beam in and out of my vision. Checking my pupils, I guess.

"Now follow the light with your eyes."

Doc moves the light up, down, right, and left. He sets the flashlight down and grabs the stethoscope. He lifts my shirt and places it on my chest. I wince, and Doc chuckles.

"Yeah, it's probably a bit cold. Sorry about that. I should have warmed it up in my hand first."

"What you should have done is hang it by the toilet seat!"

Doc laughs. "Yeah, that's a good one!"

He moves the scope around my chest and back, asking me to take some deep breaths at the same time.

"Well, your chest sounds clear. You said you don't take any medications?"

"No, not really. But I do take some meds in the fall, when my allergies start acting up."

"Allergy medications? What type?" Doc looks at me with curiosity.

"Zyrtec works really well, but the thing that really works best is Flonase."

"Zyrtec? Flonase? You sure that's what they are called?"

Doc's eyebrows are furrowed as he questions my response. Suddenly, it hits me! Zyrtec and Flonase probably weren't around in the sixties. What do I say now?

"Uh, maybe I have that wrong. They sound something like that. Anyways, I don't take them very often."

My answer does the trick. Doc eases up a bit and grabs the blood pressure cuff.

"Rest your arm on the table, and try to sit as still as possible."

He slides the cuff on my arm and starts squeezing the black rubber bulb. Instantly, the cuff tightens around my bicep. "OK, just take a deep breath and relax." He stops pumping and places the scope at the crook of my elbow, slightly under the cuff. As he slowly twists the chrome-knurled knob next to the bulb, the air begins to hiss out. I can feel the pulse in my arm as the cuff as loses air; then the sensation diminishes as the cuff goes flat.

"One twenty-five over seventy-eight. Not too bad."

He takes the cuff off my arm and puts it in the bag.

"Well, Mike, it's not like I just gave you a full physical, but you seem to be OK. Do you feel dizzy? Have a headache? Feel nauseous? Have any health issues that might explain why you fainted?"

"No, I feel fine and don't have any health issues. I mean, I have fainted before, but all were isolated incidents. One time was giving blood, and I probably fasted too long. The second time, I discovered that I was allergic to tequila."

"That's interesting!" Doc chuckles. "Never heard of that one before. How much did you drink?"

"Two drinks. Wasn't even drunk. Tequila has always given me a really bad stomach ache, though. It got worse as I got older. Anyways, when I passed out, I think it was a combination of stomach pain and anxiety."

"Anxiety?"

"Yeah, anxiety. We were with a group of friends at a restaurant, and all of us had a couple of drinks at the bar before dinner.

When we were seated for dinner, I was stuck in the middle of the table, with my back against a wall. I had no quick way out of my seat, which I didn't realize until the gut pain started. When the pain got real bad, I panicked and wanted to get some fresh air. I couldn't get out quick enough. I remember nudging my wife and telling her that I thought I might pass out. From her account, she watched my eyes roll back in my head and then I slumped over. Scared the hell out of her. Luckily, one of the guys with us was a doctor. I finally came to, and he gave me some pickle juice! Imagine that! He also sent someone to the drugstore for some Benadryl. He had me laying on my back, with my feet up on a chair. Quite embarrassing, to be honest."

"Well I'll be damned. Good move on the pickle juice," Doc says.

I nod in agreement.

"Fortunately, I had my annual physical the following week, and the doctor thought it might be an allergy to the agave root. I asked him what I should do, and he told me to not drink tequila anymore!"

"Sounds like he diagnosed the hell out of that one!"

We both have a good laugh.

Doc takes the stethoscope off his neck, wraps it up gently, and places it in the black bag, snapping it shut. He then reaches over and grabs my wool sweater, handing it to me.

"You might as well put this back on."

"Thanks."

I stand up and start to put one arm into the sleeve.

"Are you hunting up here with anyone?" he asks.

As I slide the wool over my head, I contemplate how to answer Doc's question without making him suspicious. Suddenly, the door to the cabin opens and two men walk in, dressed in deer-hunting garb and holding rifles. Looking confused, they both stop and stare at us.

"Uh, did we interrupt something, Doc?"

The other guy laughs, then says, "Shit, Doc, you even been out hunting?"

Doc scowls at them and replies, "You jackasses—it's not what you think. Did one of you clowns shoot one, or did you just wander around in the woods for the last few hours?"

I can't help but stare at these two guys in sheer disbelief— one that I only recall from old photos, and the other that I would come to know better than my own grandfather.

CHAPTER 14

ONE-SHOT CHARLIE

The short, wiry guy on the right gives Doc the middle finger, while the other one looks down and shakes his head.

The short, wiry guys says, "Unfortunately, we didn't, but Charlie did. Did you see it?"

Doc stands up. "No. Really?"

"Yeah. It's hanging in his yard. You didn't see it? How could you miss it? You walked right by it!"

"Well, I kind of got distracted." Doc motions to me. "Guys, this is Mike.... Hell, I don't even know your last name, Mike."

Oh shit, I can't say my real last name. They'll all recognize it! I got it—I'll use my middle name.

"It's, uh, Kenneth."

The wiry guy steps forward with an outstretched hand.

"Nice to meet you, Mike. Mott Lehman. By the way, your last name's a first name." He smirks.

"Yeah, so I've been told. Nice to meet you, Mott."

I can already tell that this guy is a character. The other person steps forward. He's a bit taller, a little heavier, and I'd guess in his late thirties.

"Pleasure to meet you, Mike. I'm Doyle Lehman," he says as he extends his hand.

As I shake Doyle's hand, memories flood back into my brain, recalling his firm handshake, his warm smile, and the perpetual twinkle in his eyes. Could this really be him?

"You guys family?" I ask, already knowing the answer.

Doyle looks at Mott, then back at me, and says, "Don't you see the resemblance?"

"Yeah, I think so," I reply, even though I see no resemblance at all.

"So, who's the father and who's the son?" Mott asks.

Doyle nudges Mott. "Seriously?!"

Mott laughs.

Doc says, "Let's go take a look. Is Charlie still over there?"

"Yeah, we just talked to him. He was pretty excited. He told Dad it was one of the nicest bucks he's ever shot."

"Hey Mike, do you want to tag along?"

"Sure!"

Doc and I grab our jackets, and the four of us head across the road to Charlie's place. As we walk, it's hard not to keep staring at Doyle. My mom and dad were good friends with Doyle and his wife, Jean. I remember as a kid going over to their house and seeing all of these cuckoo clocks. I was fascinated by them. Doyle knew this, and he would wind the hands around on a couple to make them chirp. His eyes would light up because he knew I loved it! They had all kinds of neat stuff in that house, including some games I would always play. One was called Shoot the Moon. You moved two metal rails back and forth, and a steel ball would be propelled uphill as you attempted to land it in the furthest slot and score the most points. That game was so addictive!

But my best memories of Doyle were golfing with him. My dad and Doyle were partners, and I would fill in for my dad when he couldn't make it. I was usually home from college, on summer break. We had some really good conversations on the course. It was special spending time with him, since he was so close to my grandpa. Unfortunately, I really never got to spend time with my grandpa like that…well, until now, I guess. I must be dreaming.

"So where are you from, Mike?"

Doyle's question snaps me out of my deep thoughts.

"Uh, Belmont, north of Grand Rapids about ten miles. Near Rockford."

"I've heard of that. I live in Montrose, almost straight east from you on M-57."

"Yeah, it's about five miles south of M-57, to be exact."

"How long you been coming up here?" Doyle asks.

"Fifteen years."

"Wow, that's quite a long time. Shot many deer?"

"Not as many as you might think—only two. Lots more deer to shoot down state, but I like coming up here better. There's something magical about the UP."

Doyle nods his head. "Yep, I know exactly what you mean. That's why we come up here, too. Your worries just melt away."

We walk into the driveway, and on the pole next to the house is a nice buck. Suddenly, the door to the house pops open and three guys come out, all wearing flannel shirts and bibs. They appear to be in their forties. One guy has a big smile on his face.

"Is that a dandy or what?" he says, grinning ear to ear.

"Yeah, that's a humdinger, Charlie," says Doc. "Eight point?"

"Yep, sure is! Shot it at seven thirty this morning over there where Mike Boddy usually hunts. He didn't make it up this year, so I figured I would hunt there. Actually, I saw two bucks. The other one was a monster, but I didn't have a decent shot, so I took this one. The other guy bolted off over there."

Charlie points in the direction where I was hunting.

"Well, that's some consolation prize," says Doyle.

"Hey, I think I saw that monster buck!" I blurt out.

Everyone looks at me.

Doc quickly chimes in, "Oh, by the way, this is Mike."

Charlie reaches out to shake my hand. "Nice to meet you, Mike. I'm Charlie. These are my brothers, Winnie and Leo."

"Hi guys, nice to meet you," I say as I shake their hands.

"Did you get a shot at it?" Leo asks, with his eyes wide open and eyebrows arched high.

"No, I didn't. I actually fell asleep, and he woke me up coming through. When I was getting my gun into position, the strap buckle must have clanked on something, and he bolted. I never got a shot off. Gosh, I don't think I've ever seen a deer that big."

Disappointed sighs come from everyone, except Mott.

"Sleeping in the woods? Well that will teach you a lesson!"

Winnie shoots a glance at Mott, rolling his eyes. "Well look who's talking! You must have forgotten about the time Doyle found you sleeping in your blind, and he shot his gun to wake you up. You were so startled, you peed your pants!"

"I did not!"

Everyone one laughs, and Mott's face turns red.

"Is this your place?" I ask Charlie.

"Yeah, but I'm not living here. I've got a little bit of work to do on it yet. Currently, I'm living in town with my wife and kids. During hunting season, us guys pitch a tent and stay out here for the week."

Charlie glances over his shoulder, and sure enough, there is a pretty good sized canvas tent, complete with what looks like a wood-burning heater. The light-blue Chevy sedan is parked next to the tent.

"Did you take the tenderloins out?" Doyle asks, peeking inside the chest cavity.

"First thing! Going to cook them over the campfire tonight. You guys can eat with us if you'd like."

"I think Doc's got dinner planned already, and we don't want to hurt his feelings. You know how he is about planning the meals up here," replies Mott.

Doc grins wide and boasts, "We will be having pork chops, with sautéed apples, baked yams, green beans, cornbread, and for dessert, pumpkin pie."

The group nods in approval, including me. I have no idea how long it's been since breakfast, and I sure as hell didn't have lunch, so I'm pretty hungry. Before I know it, I'm telling Doc how good that sounds.

"Man, I love pumpkin pie! My wife makes it every year for my birthday."

Mott says, "Who the heck eats pumpkin pie for their birthday? You're supposed to eat a cake!"

I laugh at Mott's statement, since it's not all that far from the truth.

"Yeah, I suppose it is a bit weird, but I really like pumpkin pie. And since my birthday is close the Thanksgiving, I get to eat it twice in one week."

"When's your birthday?" Doyle asks.

"The eighteenth," I say, with slight hesitation.

"Damn, that's in a couple of days," Doc says. "Speaking of food, you're welcome to eat with us tonight, unless you have other plans."

"Sure! That sounds great, as long as I'm not imposing too much on you guys."

I look at Doyle and Mott, to see if they are OK with Doc's offer. Both nod their heads in approval.

"So Charlie, give us the story on this one," Doc says, gesturing at the buck.

"Well, I got to my blind about six. The main shooting lane is east from the blind, overlooking a small swale, about fifty yards out. A few weeks ago, I noticed the deer were going through that area, so that's why I put the blind there. Also saw some huge rubs on the same path. Anyways, about seven, a couple of does wander through. They didn't spend much time on the bait pile, because they seemed nervous about something. They kept looking back behind them, like something was there. Then they spooked and ran off."

"Oh boy, here he comes!" Mott says.

"Yeah, I was thinking the same thing, and sure enough, within ten minutes, I could hear something crashing through the woods, like a bull in a china shop. Then I saw him, through the brush! Head down, sniffing the ground, moving right along. He was on a mission, if you know what I mean."

"I'm sure they knew what was coming!" says Mott, excited by the story.

"You'd be running from this guy, too, if you were a doe! Anyways, I got my gun up, thumbed the safety, and pointed it right down the shooting lane where he was headed. I'd have a clean, broadside shot. Then, at the last minute, he made a turn and disappeared back into the woods! It's almost as if he knew what was in store for him."

"So that wasn't this one?" Doyle asks, touching the buck.

"No, it wasn't."

"All be damned. You must have been devastated!"

"You can't imagine. My heart was pumping like crazy. I've never had buck fever like that. But I can tell you, he was every bit of a ten pointer."

"Holy smokes!" says Mott.

"Then, not long after I set my gun back down, I heard something else busting through the woods. I'll be damned if it wasn't another buck! He wasn't as big as the first one, but hey, I sure wasn't about to complain. So, same thing, I got my gun up and waited for him to come across the opening. As soon as he popped into the clear, I gave a little whistle and he stopped. I dropped him right in his tracks. Just like that. One shot."

"And that's why we call him 'One-Shot Charlie'!" says Doc.

Entranced by his story, everyone gazed up at the buck. I think we were all trying to imagine what it was like for Charlie this morning. Wow, what a story. And that monster buck was still out there!

Honk! Honk!

Startled, we all turn around to watch a drab green pickup turn into the driveway. From my perspective, it's a forty-year-old Chevy with a step-side bed, but to these guys, it's probably just a few years old. As the truck gets closer, two figures are visible in the cab. They park the truck, and I notice the words *Conservation Dept.*, stenciled in white letters on the door. Two guys get out, wearing heavy, drab green jackets and Stetsons. The driver is a skinny little feller, about five-foot-five. He removes his hat, sporting a high and tight crew cut. He spits on the ground as he shuts the door to the truck, takes out a hankie from his back pocket, and wipes his mouth. As he starts walking over to us, he shoves the hankie back into his pocket. The other guy is much taller, probably six-three, and about a hundred pounds heavier than the skinny guy—a big bear of a guy, with red hair. He shuts the door, grabs his holster belt with both hands to give it a little adjustment, and also approaches.

Skinny guy gets to the deer, and says, "Winnie, Leo, how you guys doing? Staying out of trouble?"

"Who, us, stay out of trouble? Why would we do that?" Leo replies.

Skinny guy rolls his eyes and then pats Charlie on the back.

"So, that's the buck, huh? We heard through the grapevine you shot one this morning."

"Yeah, this is it. Pretty nice, huh? Eight pointer. Nice spread too. Shot it about seven thirty over by Boddy's place."

"One shot?" Skinny guy's eyebrows arch up as he asks Charlie the question.

"What do you think?"

Skinny guy grunts something that I cannot understand, and Charlie smiles. One-Shot Charlie. It guess it does have a ring to it. Then, I chuckle a bit. I wonder if I should tell Charlie what it really means to be a one-shot. Nah, I don't want to rain on his parade.

Big Bear asks, "Doesn't Johnny Schultz hunt Boddy's place? He's going to be mad as a hornet when he finds out that you shot one on his hunting spot!"

Charlie frowns at Big Bear. "He didn't make it up this year. Besides, Johnny's shot enough damn deer up here. It's about time he left a few of them for us. And if he was here, I'd rub his face in it, being he's such a self-proclaimed big-game hunter!"

Leo and Winnie bust out laughing after that statement.

"Actually, I missed on a monster that came through about five minutes before this guy. By my count, it was a ten point. Had my gun up, waiting to get a clear shot, and it suddenly made a quick turn back into the thick brush. I never had a chance at it. Both bucks were chasing does, I figure. They were as nervous as hell! Heads on a swivel, kept looking all around, and tails twitching like they were on high alert. I think that the big boy had some plans for those does, if you know what I mean. The smaller buck was probably going to bat cleanup. Mike saw the same monster later in the day, we think."

Charlie points at me as he says my name. I proceed to tell the officers how I fell asleep in my blind and woke up to see the big boy staring right at me, and how I scared him off by fumbling for my gun, making too much noise.

"You don't look familiar. You from around here?" Big Bear asks.

"No, from Grand Rapids area. Name's Mike Kenneth. Nice to meet you, officer. You must be with the DNR?" I say as I hold out my hand to shake his.

Big Bear looks confused. "Nice to meet you, Mike. Red McDonald. What the heck is the DNR?"

"The Department of Natural Resources," I reply back, confused.

Red scratches his cheek, looks at skinny guy, then back at me. "Never heard of any DNR. We work for the Department of Conservation. Where did you say you're from?"

"Grand Rapids area…well, actually, Belmont, north of Grand Rapids."

I feel a bit of a panic, confused by Red's DNR statement. Maybe it didn't exist in 1960? But they are conservation officers. Isn't it the same thing? I guess I should just change the subject real quick. I make eye contact with skinny guy, and he reaches out to shake my hand.

"Nice to meet you, Mike. I'm Marty Newberg," he says with a smile.

I can see small bits of tobacco in his teeth, which would explain the spit and wipe after he got out of the truck. It would appear that Officer Newberg likes a little pinch between his cheek and gum.

I smile back. "Nice to meet you, Officer Newberg."

Marty guffaws, "Oh for Pete's sake, just call me Marty."

Marty looks at Doyle, Doc, and Mott. "You guys have any success?"

Mott replies, "Nope. Both Doyle and I haven't even seen a buck."

"I've only seen a couple of does, but no bucks," Doc adds.

"That's too bad. The deer count was high this summer, so we figured quite a few bucks would be taken. Ah, maybe your luck will change and you'll nab that big one those two saw," Marty says, looking at me and Charlie.

"That sure would be dandy," says Mott.

Doyle looks down at his watch and says to his dad, "Along that same subject, it's just about four. We need to get going if we're hunting tonight."

Mott nods and replies that he's probably right. Marty and Red mention that they need to get going too, say their good-byes, and drive off. We congratulate Charlie again and head back to the cabin. As we cross the tracks, I notice that the sun is getting low on the horizon. This is always the prettiest time of the day here. The guys will probably have about ninety minutes to hunt, if they hurry.

CHAPTER 15

SUNSET

"**A**re you guys going back out?" Mott hollers from his room. "Nah, I'm going to stay behind and get dinner going," Doc replies.

"I'm going to pass, too," I say.

Now that I think about it, I'm pretty darn tired. The last couple hours have been exhausting for me, trying to make sense of this entire situation. Is this a spectacular, vivid dream, or am I really here in the year 1960? How do I tell? It feels real. I mean, I've heard of time travel, but as far as I know, nobody has done it. How would you tell someone that you thought you traveled back in time? They would think you are crazy. The weird part is that I'm starting to feel comfortable, because it feels so real. Hanging around with Doc, Mott, and Doyle is just like being up here with the normal gang. But, if this isn't a dream, I'm going to have to figure out how to get back to where I came from. In the meantime, do I need to be careful not to say or do something that might alter the course of history? Could it have detrimental effects, like me not being born, or meeting my wife, or having kids?! I mean, that's what they always talk about in the movies when someone travels back into time. You don't want to mess up how things actually happened. Damn, I know enough things about Doyle and my grandfather that if I told them any of it, they might do something different going forward in life. I know when and how both of them die. I could tell them things that they could profit from, like that Joe Namath and the New York Jets will beat the Colts in Super Bowl III. That was a huge upset. I mean, if this is really November of 1960, Kennedy just won the election. I could tell them that he is going to be assassinated in three years by a man named Lee Harvey Oswald in Dallas! Shit, NASA is going to land Armstrong and Aldrin on the moon in nine years! Oh, and let's not forget about one immediate problem: Where am I going to stay tonight?

I can't just leave, because I have nowhere to go. They can't drive me downtown to grab a room at the motel, because what would I pay with? Credit cards that don't exist? Currency that hasn't been printed? They would think my money's counterfeit. I subtly reach back and touch my wallet, making sure I still have it. I'll have to make sure I keep that thing out of these guys' hands. I have all kinds of stuff in there that would cause suspicion. I take a deep breath. OK, I need to calm down. Worrying about this isn't helping me right now. I look over at Doc. He is rummaging through one of the kitchen cabinets.

He turns and says, "So you're not going back out?"

"No, I'm pretty tired, and actually, to be honest, I think that I'm having some memory issues. I can't remember how I got up here or where I'm staying. All I know is that I woke up in my blind this afternoon, saw a monster buck staring at me, and started to panic because I didn't know where I was. I finally calmed myself down and used a bit of common sense to get out of the woods. Then, I ran into you."

Doyle and Mott, on a mission to get back out hunting, seem oblivious to what I just said. They are dressed and heading for the door, guns in hand. Both say good-bye and are gone, their conversation fading as they head toward Huckleberry.

"Jeez, they don't have much time left to hunt. When does the official hunt time end today?"

"I think it's about five thirty or so," Doc says.

He walks over to the shelf and digs out a hunting pamphlet. "Actually, five forty."

Doc reaches for the radio and tunes it to a station playing some jazz. It sounds like Louis Armstrong. It's AM radio, with that unmistakable interference noise.

"You didn't tell me about your memory issues," Doc says as he sets the radio back on the shelf.

"I wanted to mention it, but by the time you finished checking me out, the boys walked in; then we went over to see Charlie's buck. I guess I got distracted."

"So can you be more specific about it?"

"Like I said, I can't recall how I got up here. But on the other hand, things look somewhat familiar."

"Like what?"

"Well, everything. But at the same time, things look different. It's rather difficult to describe the feeling. Kind of like I'm in some sort of a time warp."

I can't believe I just said that.

"Hmm, that's quite interesting. Hey, on the way to Charlie's, I heard you tell Doyle you live near Grand Rapids, in Belmont."

"Yeah, I did say that, and I'm pretty sure that's true."

Doc chuckles, and says, "You're pretty sure that's true?"

I laugh and say, "That doesn't sound very convincing, does it?"

"No, not really. Do you recall if you know anyone up here?"

"Not that I can think of right now."

"Interesting."

"That's the second time you said that."

Doc laughs again. "Yeah, I guess it is."

He stares off in the distance for what seems like a few minutes. I try to get a sense of what he's thinking. He doesn't look concerned, and if he is, he doesn't show it.

Doc finally says, "Maybe you fell and bumped your head? That could explain a few things. I don't want to scare you, but the other possibility is that you had a stroke. But, you don't exhibit any signs of a stroke. Does your head hurt, like you fell and hit it on something?"

I run my fingers through my hair. No bumps, not sore. I look at my hands and don't see any blood.

"Not really. I feel like a hundred bucks, to be honest with you. Just a bit tired, that's all."

"Well, I could drive you to the hospital right now, but if you're OK with just staying here, I'll keep an eye on you. I'm figuring your memory will come back pretty quick, and if it doesn't, well, we can make a decision later about what to do."

"Sounds like a plan to me."

Doc turns back to the cabinet and grabs a couple of pots. He places them on the stove and turns back to the cabinet to dig some more. Then he stops and looks directly at me.

"I have to admit, I have this strange feeling that we have met before. It's the weirdest thing. There's something very familiar about you, but I can't quite put my finger on it."

Oh really, I say to myself. *You think I look familiar? Well maybe it's because my mom is your daughter!* Afraid to tell him the truth, I redirect his last statement.

"Well, I've heard that from other people before. I must have that type of a face or something."

Doc grabs a shallow baking pan, shuts the door to the cabinet, and puts the pan on the counter.

"Yeah that must be it. Maybe you just have one of those faces.... So, hey, do you like to cook?"

"Yeah, I do!"

"Would you mind peeling and slicing those apples? Make sure to take the cores out of them. Do about six or seven," Doc says.

He walks toward the door and disappears outside, reappearing a few minutes later, carrying a pale-green Coleman cooler. It looks like an antique, but in perfect condition! The base is white, and the metal is smooth, except for the diamond pattern embossed on the cover. On the front lower-left side is a white diamond-shaped placard, with *Coleman* written in white and a red background. The familiar chrome latch rests on the front and the handles on the side. A good design never changes! He places the cooler on the dinner table, flips the latch, and pulls out a large package. He unwraps some brown butcher's paper to reveal six very thick pork chops.

"Those sure do look good!"

Doc turns to me and grins. "Yeah, I bought them at a meat store in Cheboygan. Great selection. One of our regular stops on the way up is a restaurant called the Carnation. The steaks are incredible, and we found out that the butcher across the street supplies the restaurant. So, we checked them out and have been buying meat from them every time we come up."

"Damn, they must be an inch-and-a-half thick! How you going to cook them?"

Doc picks up one of the pork chops and looks at it lovingly.

"Season with a little salt and pepper, sear them in the skillet with a little butter, and finish them in the oven. You don't want to dry them out. It's like shoe leather if you do. You have to walk that fine line between trichinosis and tenderness when cooking. Hey, when you get done with those apples, put them in this sauté pan right here."

I laugh at the trichinosis comment as I start to cut up the apples. I tell that to my kids all the time. Now I know where it comes from.

"Sure, no problem. Anything else I can do?"

"There are a couple cans of green beans and yams in the trunk. Also, a couple boxes of cornbread mix," Doc says while seasoning the chops.

I grimace. Green beans in a can? Yuk.

"Green beans in a can? Don't you have any fresh ones?"

Doc looks over at me, a bit perturbed by my statement.

"Just where the hell do you think you're going to get fresh green beans in November?"

"The grocery store, I guess. In the produce area?"

Doc chuckles. "Green bean season was over months ago. I don't know what store you are thinking about, but there aren't any fresh green beans in the store where I get my groceries."

"Yeah, I guess you're right. What the hell was I thinking?" I reply.

I guess I was really thinking about the fresh green beans that I grabbed at Meijer last week for deer camp. Well, that would be last week in November 2016! It must be that in the sixties, fresh produce was seasonal. That would make sense.

I finish slicing the apples, put them in the saucepan, and wander outside. I pop the trunk on Doc's Caddy and rifle through the brown paper grocery bags to gather up the yams, green beans, and cornbread mix. I examine one of the cans. They look like they came out of a time warp too, with their old-fashioned labeling. I walk back inside.

"Hey Doc, how you going to cook the yams?"

"I think the directions are on the can. Use this."

Doc hands me a shallow baking dish.

I look at the back of the can, and sure enough, there are the directions. In a saucepan, melt one half cup of butter, two-thirds cup of brown sugar, and two-thirds cup of syrup from the can. I need a can opener. I turn to ask Doc for one, and suddenly, just like he was reading my mind, he tosses one over. I open the cans of yams and dump them into the baking dish.

"Where do you keep the butter and brown sugar?"

"Brown sugar is on top of the cabinet here. Butter is over by the window sill. Here's a small sauce pan," Doc says, handing me the pan.

I put one stick of butter in the pan, dump in the brown sugar and syrup, and light the burner. Next to me, Doc has the chops all seasoned and ready for the skillet.

Doc checks off, "The chops are ready to brown. The yam sauce is heating up. The apples are cooking. Oh, let's get the cornbread batter ready. We probably just need one box."

He goes over to the table, grabs a box of mix, and looks at the back of it. I watch him as he opens the package, dumps it into a mixing bowl, and adds eggs and milk. He grabs a fork and mixes the batter with quick flicks of his wrist. I glance at my watch.

"What time do you think the boys will be back?"

"I'm thinking about six or so. At five forty, it's so dark in the woods that you can't see what you're shooting at. Now that I think of it, I don't remember anyone shooting a deer up here in the evening. Lots of issues if you shoot one at dusk. You better hope that you drop it right there; otherwise, you're tracking it. Then, you're going to be cleaning it with the coyotes looking over your shoulder. Personally, I would rather just hang out here and get dinner going."

I laugh. "Yeah, I feel the same way. I never liked the idea of shooting a deer in the evening up here. Speaking of Mott and Doyle, how did you meet them?"

"When my wife and I moved to Montrose, they were our first friends. Doyle was just a pup, eighteen years old, and heading to the army. Mott was running the hardware store in town. Mott is about eight years older than me, and Doyle is about seven years younger. I'm right in the middle. We all get along, wives included. We like to play cards, and Doyle and Mott enjoy hunting. We do a little bowling too."

"You guys come up here quite a bit?"

"Lately we have, but prior to that it was a bit sporadic. It was a pain in the ass before the bridge, especially during deer season. All those cars lined up for miles in Mackinaw City, waiting to get on the ferry. What a mess. One year, I didn't want to wait, so I talked the boys into driving through Chicago and up the other side of Lake Michigan instead of taking that damn ferry."

"You're kidding! How much time did that take?" I say laughing.

"Too long. However, we did find a few good places to eat!" Doc says with a twinkle in his eye.

"Just like the Carnation, huh? I think I'm starting to see a pattern here, Doc."

"Well you got me there. I do love to eat, no doubt about that. Nothing like a good meal with good friends."

"I going to guess that you guys bird hunt up here, too?"

"Yeah, grouse and woodies. We come up almost every weekend in the fall. Actually, if you look on the walls, we document some of our excursions—something we started doing a few years ago. You ought to grab a pencil and write some stuff before you leave. Oh shoot, that reminds me. Stay right there!"

Doc stops mixing, sets the bowl down, and walks into the front room. I look at the wall next to the dinner table and see the writing. I wander closer to have a better look. Something about breaking camp on November 13, 1958, forty-three degrees, one thirty in the morning. Signed by Doc. Hmm, I don't ever recall seeing this one, but maybe it's still there and has just faded over the years. I know that some of the penciled stuff on the door is hard to read, and that stuff was written in the mid-sixties. Doc appears again, holding something in his hand.

"What do you have there?" I ask him.

"A camera! We're going to take a picture. Grab the toilet seat on the wall," Doc says, with a big grin on his face.

Oh my gosh, how could I forget! The tradition of every visitor to the Trout Lake cabin—a photograph of them holding up the toilet seat with their head peeking through the hole. All of these photos have been assembled into an album up here. I grab the toilet seat, warm from the heat coming off the Duo-Therm, and look at Doc, knowing all too well what I am going to be asked to do.

Doc is still smiling as he explains the procedure.

"So, a few years ago, we came up with this idea that everybody who visits this place has to have their photograph taken with their head poking through the seat."

Doc simulates the pose, using his hands like he is holding up an imaginary seat.

"Just like this. It's just a stupid thing that became tradition."

"So, you want me to put my face near this thing?" I say, examining the seat closely.

Doc laughs.

"Don't worry, I'm a doctor. If you get something, I'll just give you a shot of penicillin. So, hold it up there."

I put the seat up to my head and stick my face into the hole.

"OK, give me a big smile!"

A flash pops.

"Nice one! Hey, you got something on your cheek!" Doc says, placing a finger on his cheek.

I quickly swipe at my cheek and look at my hand, but don't see anything. Doc is now laughing.

"Just kidding! You should have seen the look on your face!"

"Real funny."

I hang the seat back on the nail. Doc sets the camera down and resumes mixing the cornbread. He looks into the bowl and frowns.

"I don't think this is going to be enough."

He sets down the bowl and reaches for the other box. He opens the contents, dumps it in, adds some more milk, another egg, and starts mixing again.

"Grab that baking dish right there, and rub some of that bacon grease into the pan, if you don't mind," Doc instructs, pointing to the window.

I grab a small glass jar of what looks like bacon grease. I look around for some paper towels but don't see any.

"What you looking for?"

"Some paper towels."

Doc points over toward the door, "They're over there, on the shelf."

I walk over, tear one off, dip it into the grease, and slather the baking dish with the creamy white substance. I can feel my arteries clogging up right now! I set the dish down on the table, and Doc fills it with the batter.

"I think we are set. Just need to get the beans on the burner, but that shouldn't take long." He glances down at his watch. "Five-thirty. Let's get the chops started."

Doc lights the oven, messes with the temperature dial, and then lights one of the top burners, placing the iron skillet on top. He bends over, lifts the skillet slightly, and adjusts the burner flame to his satisfaction. A few minutes later, the chops are sizzling on the hot cast iron and the yams are in the oven. Soon after, the chops enter the oven and Doc has the green beans in a small saucepan on the stove, cooking away. The smell of the apples makes me drool. I lift the lid a bit to peek. He must have added some butter, brown sugar, and cinnamon. About quarter to six, Doc slides the cornbread into the oven and turns the heat down on the beans and apples. A maestro in the kitchen! I just sit back and watch, but I feel like something's missing. Then it hits me….

"Hey Doc, you have anything to drink around here? I could use a little nip of something."

"Well we really aren't big drinkers, but I think there is some beer in the cooler, and whiskey and Grand Marnier over there on the shelf."

I take a peek in the cooler and grab a red can with a black, angled label. My mind instantly jumps back in time, to when I was a kid. Carling Black Label. Yikes! Wincing, I look over at the shelf and see a familiar purple velvet pouch with gold strings. Crown Royal. That's more like it! Somebody has some class up here. I put the beer back into the cooler and grab the liquor.

"The glasses are over here, and there is a separate bag of ice in the cooler. Not a big fan of Black Label, huh?"

I look at Doc and grimace. "I'm not so sure about that stuff."

Doc laughs.

"Black Label's not one of the better brands out there, but Mottsie really likes it. While you're over there, pour me a jigger-full of Grand Marnier, neat, if you don't mind."

I grab two tumblers, pouring the orange-tasting liqueur into one of them and handing it to Doc.

"Thanks!"

Giving him a warm smile and nod, I grab a handful of ice out of the cooler, drop it into the glass, and pour some Crown Royal. Now that's what I'm talking about! A predinner toddy at Trout Lake is a necessity!

I turn to Doc and raise my glass. "Cheers!"

Doc smiles back and says in agreement, "Cheers!"

Clink! I take a long sip on the Crown and smile at my grandpa. Could I really be here right now with him, having a drink?

Doc takes a sip, swallows, and says, "Are you sure we haven't met somewhere?"

I laugh.

"No Doc, I'm pretty sure that we haven't met."

Suddenly, we hear boots stomping on the steps, and then the door opens. Mott and Doyle are back, looking like two tired dogs, but their expressions change quickly when they smell the food.

CHAPTER 16

MOTT AND DOYLE

"**I**'m guessing you guys came back empty-handed again?" Doc says.

"We didn't see a damn thing," Mott replies, clearly frustrated.

Doyle laughs and follows his dad into their room. I assume they are putting their guns away and changing into some more comfortable clothes. A few minutes later, both wander out wearing trousers, T-shirts, and I'll be darned, the same kind of slippers that Tim wears! I laugh to myself, envisioning Hugh Hefner in his famous red velvet smoking jacket, with a pipe hanging from the corner of his mouth. I can't hold back.

"Those are some damn fine slippers, guys. You both look like Hugh Hefner, but without the pipe and velvet smoking jacket."

Doc bursts out laughing. Doyle looks down at his slippers, trying to analyze what I just said, and Mott just looks at me with his mouth open, not sure what to say. Doyle is the first to speak, looking like he might cry.

"These are Parry Romeo's! They're really nice slippers. What's wrong with them?"

Mott adds, "For Christ's sake, Doyle, he's just messing with you. He has no clue about style. Didn't you see that stupid bright-orange stocking cap he was wearing today? Who the hell would wear something like that out hunting? The deer would see it from a mile away!"

Oh shit, I didn't even think about that! Blaze orange didn't come out until the mid-seventies.

"I guess you got me on that one, Mott. I never thought about it scaring off the deer."

I would like to set Mott straight, but I can't. Since the sixties, numerous studies have been done on the vision of white-tailed deer, and scientists have come to the conclusion that blue is the only color that deer might recognize. Doyle forgets about his shoes and wanders over to the stove. He opens the oven up and takes a peek.

"Oh, this really looks good, Doc. Smells good too. When's it going to be ready?"

"Right now," Doc replies.

Mott peeks over Doyle's shoulder.

"It's a good thing we bring you along to cook, Doc."

"Yeah, especially since you and Doyle are shooting so many deer!"

We all have a good laugh at that one.

Doc assembles the food while we set the table. Finally, we sit down and admire the meal before us. Pork chops with sautéed apples. Green beans, yams, and cornbread. We don't need to pass the food around, since it's only a short reach away, centered on the table. I cut into the pork chop and take a bite—it is perfectly pink and juicy. No piece of leather here! The sound of silverware clanks on porcelain, taking precedence over conversation, save for a couple of "mm's" and "oh this is so good." I guess all of us are pretty hungry! After a few bites, I glance across the table at Mott.

"So Mott, Doc said you guys have known each other for some time now?"

"Ah, let's see. We've known each other for about, what, twenty years or so?"

Doc nods his head and replies, "Moved to Montrose in January of thirty-nine, so it will be twenty-two years in a few months."

"Yeah, you're right. Man, it seems like just yesterday. Twenty-two years, hmm. Time sure does fly," Mott says, then scrapes some food up from his plate and takes a bite.

"I remember when we heard Doc was coming to town. It was big news," Doyle said.

"Dr. Farley took a job back home, in Maine. He called me and suggested that I take over his practice," Doc said. "I had heard of Montrose but had never been there. Just knew it was south of Saginaw and north of Flint—that's about it. I was working at Saginaw Osteopathic at the time. Remember when we first met, Mottsie? At Schramm's Rexall."

"That's right. You and George were having a conversation when I walked in. I was looking for some bandages because I had just cut my finger on the pipe-cutting machine. It was a stroke of luck that you were there, because I ended up needing a couple of stitches."

"Who's George?" I ask.

"That would be George Schramm, the pharmacist and owner," says Doc.

"You cut it on a pipe threader?" I ask Mott.

"Yeah. Just got it a few weeks prior, so we hadn't used it much. I was learning by trial and error, if you know what I mean. Mr. Baxter came in one day, and wanted some pipe cut and threaded. I was having a hell of a time with the thread die."

"Mean ole Mr. Baxter. He sure was a crotchety, old coot," Doyle says.

The three of them laugh.

Mott continues, "Got my finger caught in the damn thing while the chuck was turning. Those thread dies are sharp little sons of bitches. Took a bite right out of me."

"That must have hurt like hell."

"It sure as heck didn't tickle!"

"What type of business are you in?" I ask, already knowing the answer.

"I own a hardware store. Had it for about thirty years."

I cut another hunk of meat and add some apples before putting it into my mouth. Man, this is good. The food on everyone's plate is disappearing fast.

"Did you grow up there?" I ask Mott.

"No, in Flint. I moved here in the early thirties, after I bought the store. I was managing a chain of retail hardware stores in Flint for this company called Morgan Brothers. You ever heard of them?"

I want to tell him yes. I remember when the Morgan Brothers sales rep would visit my dad at his hardware store and take orders for supplies. I was linked to the Lehman clan in more than one way. My dad's store was about eight miles away, and he and Doyle would often refer customers to each other if they didn't have something they wanted. Occasionally, my dad would send me over to Lehman Hardware to drop some stuff off or pick it up.

I'd take an International Harvester Scout that had a four-speed, manual transmission. I think the official color was "Glacier Blue." I remember the first time I took it. I wasn't an expert on driving a manual transmission, but I wasn't intimidated. Dad showed me the shift pattern and warned me about the steering. Boy, was he right! It liked to wander all over the road. Pieces of wood and tractor parts would roll side to side in the bed of the truck as I drove. The pickup smelled of grease, oil, and dirt. The seats were vinyl, and the floor was painted steel with a grungy rubber mat. It was mainly used by the mechanics going out on call to repair the large tractors. The hardware store was part of an IH dealership that my dad owned with three other partners. Anyways, I would make the short drive on M-13 from New Lothrop to Montrose, and spend the next half hour catching up with Doyle, Tim, and Del. Doyle's mom, Macye, would be on the mezzanine that overlooked the store. I think that she took care of the books. I remember going up there a few times and seeing paperwork piled high up over the place. They say that smells bring back memories, and to this day, I can still remember the smell of Lehman Hardware—specifically the oiled hardwood floors. I never had the chance to meet Mott until today. He died the year before I was born, in 1963.

"Nope, never heard of Morgan Brothers," I lie through my teeth.

"Ah. Anyways, they repossessed the store in Montrose, then sent me over to manage it. A few years later, I bought it. Been there ever since."

I look over at Doyle, who is busy eating, not really fascinated by the story. I'm sure he has heard it a million times. I ask him if he works at the store, again knowing the answer.

"Yep, been there since I came out of the army," he replies.

"Just you two? No other family?"

Doyle stops chewing briefly and looks at Mott.

"Nope, just me and Dad."

I glance at both of them. Something was weird right there.

"Did I say something wrong?" I ask.

"No, no, you didn't. I don't have any siblings. I'm adopted."

"You know, when both of you walked through the door earlier this afternoon and said you were father and son, I lied that I saw a resemblance!"

Doyle and Mott chuckle.

"So, is there a story behind this?" I ask.

Mott says, "Well, there is a story, but I'm not sure if you would call it a good one. It's interesting, though."

"With a few twists and turns," adds Doyle.

"So, I met Doyle's mom, Macye, back in the late twenties. She had moved up here from southeast Missouri, near Kennett. At the time, General Motors was bringing up quite a few people from that area to work in their Flint factories, and her sisters were already up here. Doyle was in first grade at the time. He attended Doyle School on Saginaw Street."

"Doyle School? How much of a coincidence is that?"

"No kidding. Pretty funny, huh?" Doyle says.

Mott continues, "Macye did housekeeping and cooking for a doctor in Flint. I met her one day when she came into the store. I thought she was a pretty cute, so I asked her on a date. Been together ever since. We married in 1930, and I adopted Doyle shortly after."

"My mom was fifteen when she had me."

"Wow, that is young. So, you two must be about fifteen years apart?"

"Sixteen. Which is probably why we look so close in age. Right, Doyle?"

Doyle laughs. "Well, I guess so."

"So your mom followed her sisters up here?" I ask Doyle.

"Not really. She was actually trying to get away from my biological father. A drunk painter, no less. I'll be damned if the guy didn't follow us up here, though. Like a bad dream that keeps happening. One of these days I'll have to give him a piece of my mind."

Mott glances at Doyle and then says, "Well, fortunately, he doesn't bother us."

"Yeah, I guess you're right. He doesn't. Coincidentally, my mother is also adopted. And go figure, her father is a drunk too. A drunken Indian. Probably the reason why I don't drink much."

I look at both of them, and say, "Tough story. I'm really sorry."

Mott says, "Ah, it's no big deal. We have a pretty good life."

Doyle puts his arm around Mott and says, "Yes we do, Dad."

"So, what's this story about you having some memory issues?" Doyle asks.

"Uh, what do you mean?" I reply, caught off guard by his question.

"Well, when Dad and I were getting dressed, I heard you talking to Doc about memory issues and that's why you didn't want to go out. Something about falling asleep in the blind and then waking up wondering where you were. Is that true?"

Damn, I didn't think they heard me.

"Yeah, well, I guess I might as well toss the skunk on the porch, as they say. You probably would have eventually started asking questions about what the heck I'm still doing here."

"Well, you're right. We would have gotten to that sooner or later. I mean, when Doyle and I walked in on you and Doc, you were putting your clothes on and Doc looked like he was, well, playing doctor. No pun intended, Doc," Mott says, looking at him.

Doc and Doyle burst out laughing, and I can't stop myself from laughing either. Mott can't keep a straight face for long and soon enough joins us. That dude is quick-witted, for sure.

"Well, from what I can piece together, the last thing I remember is waking up in my blind, staring at a monster buck. He was looking at me, so I had to move slowly to grab my gun. By the time I had it in my hand, he was looking away, so I was able to get him in the crosshairs. But then, it suddenly hit me like a ton of bricks that the woods just didn't look right. Something was out of place. Off-kilter. And I must have said something out loud that startled the buck, and he bolted. It didn't matter at that point, though, because I really started to panic.."

"Jeez," says Doyle.

"So, I just sat there for a bit and calmed myself down. I think I pinched myself a few times to see if I was in a dream."

"Why don't I give you a little slap right now?" Mott suggests.

Doyle and Doc laugh, and Mott smiles.

"I think I'll pass on your offer, but thanks anyways."

"Ah, no problem. So, keep going."

"Heck, I didn't really know what to do at that point. I finally stepped out from my blind and took a look around to get my bearings. I looked at my watch, looked at the sun, you know, checked out my compass. I could hear cars driving in the distance, so I started walking in that direction. Eventually, I popped out of the woods and ended up on the road across the street. By the time I got to the tracks, I had to wait because a train was going through. Then Doc popped up behind me."

Doc says, "I guess I startled him. He turned around, stared at me for a couple of seconds, and called me 'Grandpa'!"

Lying, I say, "I'm not sure I remember saying that!"

"Well, that's what you said, and then you passed out."

Mott says, "Jesus, this is unbelievable! Called you Grandpa, and then passed out?"

"Yep, that's what he said! Turned white as a sheet, called me 'Grandpa,' and went down. Anyways, he eventually came to, and we walked over to the cabin because I wanted to make sure that he was OK. You two clowns walked in right after I finished checking him out."

Mott, looking confused, says to me, "So what do else do you remember?"

"Well, not much about coming up here at all. I don't know if I drove up by myself, came with some guys, or what. That's the frustrating thing. I know my name, where I'm from, that I think I'm married and have three kids, but nothing about coming up here. I have no idea how I got into the woods."

Mott looks at Doc and asks, "So why the heck didn't you just take him to the hospital?"

"He didn't have any obvious injuries, and I ruled out a few other things like a stroke, so I figured that I would just keep him here and eventually his memory would come back, and we could go from there. Heck, if he is still the same way tomorrow, we can run him over to the Soo or call his wife at home."

Mott looks at me with suspicion, his eyes narrowing.

"So he's staying tonight? How do we know he's not planning to do something to us?"

"Like what?" I blurt out.

"Oh for gosh sakes, Dad, come on!"

"His story sounds a bit suspicious, don't you think? He could be making the whole damn thing up. Going to slit our throats tonight while we are sleeping—take our stuff, you know."

Doc jumps in, "Are you kidding me, Mott? He doesn't look like some killer to me. And what the hell is he going to take? All we have here is guns, and they aren't worth much money."

"He could steal your Caddy!" Mott says, while pointing his finger in the direction of the car. "Get some good money for that."

Doc looks at me and says, "I guess I'll take my chances. Do you plan on slitting our throats tonight, and stealing our guns and my car?"

"Well, slitting your throats might be too messy. Maybe I'll just steal those Jerry Rodeo shoes, or whatever you call them."

"PARRY ROMEO!" Mott hollers.

Doyle and Doc crack up laughing, but Mott just sits there and looks at me, brows furrowed and eyes glaring.

Doc changes the subject quickly.

"Hey, let's get this mess cleaned up. Who wants to clean the dishes?"

"I can help with that! It's the least I can do for your hospitality."

Doyle adds, "I can give you a hand, Mike. You want to wash or dry?"

"I'll do the washing."

Doyle smiles, and says, "Sounds good to me."

Mott starts gathering dishes and piles them up at the end of the table. He is still looking at me with suspicion. The rest of the evening might be tense with Mott. Ah, maybe he will soften up a bit. I wish that there was some way that could just be honest with them, but that probably wouldn't work. I'm just going to have to just lie my way through the evening and hope that I can figure out how to get myself out of this mess—and back home where I belong, somehow! The longer that I'm here, the more likely things are to veer off in the wrong direction, and I could find myself in a heap of trouble.

CHAPTER 17

NIGHTFALL

Doyle and I chat while doing the dishes. Talking with him brings back so many memories of when he was alive. Gosh, what a weird thought. Someone dies, and then here they are again, talking to you. I want so badly to tell him about how I got here or, rather, how I *think* I got here. It's getting harder to keep it a secret. On the other hand, I'm starting to feel as though it's not going to matter if I tell them because none of this is probably real anyway. So what's the risk? I guess I'm not sure. Maybe things will become clearer later on.

The last dish is finally wiped and put away. Doyle goes outside to dump the dirty dish water, and I grab a seat next to Doc, who is sitting at the table with Mott. Both are reading magazines. Mott's drinking a Black Label.

Doc looks up and asks how I'm doing.

"Not too bad," I answer.

"I still think it would be best if you stayed here tonight, and then let's discuss what we are going to do tomorrow morning if your memory is still bad."

I look over at Mott, who is still reading.

"Are you sure that's going to be OK with him?"

Mott stops reading, looks up at me, and then looks at Doc. Doc shoots him a glance, "Yeah, he will be OK with it."

Mott grunts at Doc, and goes back to reading. I guess that means he's OK with the idea.

Doc points to my hunting pants and says, "You want to get out of those things?"

"Sure, that might be more comfortable."

"We have some extra sleeping bags and pillows in the front closet, and we have more than enough beds available in the front room. Usually, we have a few more guys up here hunting."

We walk through the doorway, and Doc points to the bed over in the corner.

"You can take that one."

"Thanks."

Doc opens up a cabinet, pulls out a sleeping bag and a pillow, and tosses it over to me. The bed is a single with a thin mattress. The metal frame is old, with a nice patina finish. It will do just fine. I sit on the bed, remove my boots, and wiggle my toes. Gosh that feels good. I slip off my suspenders and begin to remove my pants, struggling to get my left foot out of the cuff. Damn thing. I have to literally put a couple fingers inside the cuff and pry it off my heel. If I ever make it back, I will buy a new suit for next year. Hunter orange, in honor of

Mott. I chuckle to myself. Finally, my pants are removed and I'm in my thermal underwear and T-shirt.

"We'll all be in the same outfit, so no big deal. Not much of a dress code around here. Here's a pair of slippers."

Doc tosses them to me, and I check them out. Yeah, these should fit.

"Hope you're not disappointed that they aren't Perry Como's," Doc says with a smile.

"I heard that!" Mott hollers from the other room.

I laugh and say, "That's a good one."

We walk back into the other room. Doyle is over by the sink, in his thermal underwear and slippers, cleaning up with soap and a washcloth. Face, hair, underarms, then, oh dear, his butt. He mumbles something about dingle berries. I have a moment of déjà vu, and I swear I've seen a black-and-white photo of him at the sink washing his backside!

"Hey, do you want a drink?" Doc asks.

"Yeah, that sounds great."

"The same as before—whiskey on the rocks?"

"That sounds wonderful."

Doyle turns around, and says to Doc, "Hey, pour me one of those, will you? Just a shot."

Then Mott says, "Grab another beer for me, too. If I'm going to die tonight, I might as well be numb."

He looks over at me with no expression on his face. Then, he winks. I smile back and take a seat at the table. I think we are good.

"I didn't mean to act like that earlier. It's just that your story is a bit peculiar, to say the least," Mott confides.

"Yeah, you're telling me. I'm more frustrated than you know."

I take a sip of my drink as Doyle takes a seat next to Mott. Doc sits down next to me and slides Mott his beer.

"Thanks, Doc."

"No problem. Hey, you guys interested in some euchre?"

"Sure," we all say.

Doyle reaches up behind him and grabs a deck of cards from a small shelf. I watch him as he opens the carton and pulls out the cards. He sorts through them and sets the fives on the side. He then goes through the rest of the deck, putting aside four each of the nines, tens, and jacks through aces. He puts the rest of the cards in the jacket, gathers the rest up in his hand, and starts to shuffle. He looks up at me.

"Looks like we're partners, Mike."

"Yes, it does."

"First black jack deals," Doyle says, as he starts flipping cards around the table. On the second go-around, Doc gets the card.

Doc gathers all of the cards, shuffles, and deals five to each of us, in groups of twos and threes. He flips over the top card of the remaining four that are left. An ace of spades appears. I look at my cards and see all hearts and diamonds. At least I have both aces.

"Pass," I say, rapping my knuckles on the table.

Mott arranges the cards in his hand, and says, "Pick it up."

I look over at Doyle and grimace a bit. Doyle shakes his head. This is not going to be a good first hand. Doc picks up the ace and discards it.

"Looks like spades are trump, boys," Doc says.

I lay down the ace of diamonds. Mott throws down the ten of diamonds, and Doyle follows with the queen of diamonds. Doc mutters something as he throws down the king of diamonds.

Doc glances at Mott. "I sure as hell hope you have more than that!"

"Ah, we will be just fine."

I throw down the ace of hearts.

"Son of a bitch!" Mott says as he tosses down the king of hearts.

Doyle follows with the ten of clubs, and Doc throws down the jack of hearts.

"Do you smell a euchre, Doyle?"

"I think so!"

All the good cards gone, I lay down the queen of hearts.

"Well, take a whiff of this, boys!" Mott proclaims as he throws down the jack of spades.

Doyle throws down a heart, Doc follows with a spade. Mott pulls in the cards and tosses out the left bower. Doyle follows with another heart, Doc throws a spade, and I finish with another heart. Mott then tosses out the queen of clubs.

"Well this one doesn't mean crap, because Doc still has the ace," Doyle says as he tosses the ace of clubs to the center of the table. Doc slaps the ace of spades down, and I follow up with another red card. First hand to team Doc and Mott.

Mott and Doc slide the cards over to me. I shuffle, deal, and then flip over the jack of clubs. Sweet. Mott passes, but Doyle orders it up. I look down at my cards and smile. One off-suit ace and a couple of clubs. We take all five hands and two points. Mott's deal.

"So Doc, you said you moved to Montrose about twenty years ago?" I ask.

Doc picks up his cards as Mott deals and rearranges them in his hand.

"Yep."

"Where are you originally from?" I ask, looking at my own cards.

Doyle knocks on the table. Doc does the same. I pass too. Mott picks up the card, which is the king of hearts. He must have the right bower and an ace. Maybe shorthanded with his discard.

"Quincy, Illinois."

"Where did you go to med school?"

"Missouri. Kirksville College of Osteopathic Medicine. When I finished up, I interned in Carson City at the Osteopathic Hospital. After that was done, I went to Saginaw Osteopathic Hospital."

"How did you end up in Michigan, not somewhere in Illinois?"

"It was one of the internship options. I had never been to Michigan but heard that the hunting was pretty good, so I thought I might as well take the position."

So you never went back to Quincy?"

"Sure, but just to visit. Not sure why I didn't move back. I guess that I was too busy to think about it, and then next thing I know, I'm finishing up in Saginaw and taking the job in Montrose."

Mott takes the first hand with the right bower, grabs the cards, and throws down the ace of diamonds. Yep, just like I thought. Doyle follows suit and so does Doc. However, I lay down the jack of diamonds and grab the cards. Mott gives me a dirty look, and Doyle slaps his hand down on the table. I throw down the ace of spades, but Mott takes the hand with his king of hearts. Mott then follows with the queen of hearts and takes the point.

"Lucky on that one, Dad."

"Not really," Mott says as he slides the cards over to Doyle.

"So, you moved to Montrose right after Saginaw Osteopathic?"

"Pretty much. I got to know Dr. Farley when I was in Saginaw, and when he decided to move back to Maine, he gave me a call to see if I was interested in buying the practice. The only hitch was that I was engaged at the time, and I had to make sure that my fiancée was OK with the move."

"I assume she was?"

"Yeah. Her first impression of Montrose was Main Street. She loved the big trees that lined it with all that shade. She thought that it gave a beautiful look to the town. And the houses. They were all well kept. Seems like that was just yesterday."

Doyle deals out the cards and turns over a king of spades. I have the ace and ten in spades. We all pass, and I hope that Doyle has something and picks it up, which he does. Doc throws out the king of hearts, and not having a heart, I trump it with the ten of spades. It takes the hand, and I lead with a heart. Doyle takes it with the left bower and throws out the right. We eventually win another point. The score is tied at five apiece. Doc shuffles and deals again. He turns up the jack of spades.

"Way to go, Doc!" Mott says.

"So how come you chose to be an osteopath instead of an MD?"

"That's a good question. I guess that I liked the holistic aspect of being an osteopath, and that there are different ways to treat people instead of just prescribing drugs. You heal the soul and the spirit. Don't get me wrong, I do prescribe drugs, but there is usually a root cause that can be fixed without the use of drugs. I like that challenge."

"Pass. So is Kirksville a pretty good school?"

Mott passes, along with Doyle. Doc slides his discard under the deck and picks up the bower.

"One of the best, actually. It was the first osteopathic medical school in the world. Started back in the late 1800s."

"Darn, that's pretty impressive," I say, then lay down the ace of clubs. I assume this one will make the round, but it doesn't, as Doc throws down a low spade. He follows with the both bowers. Team Doc and Mott eventually take all of the hands and win two points. We play on for the next fifteen minutes, and eventually, Doyle and I come back to win the game by two points.

Doc suddenly says, "Damn, we forgot about the pie! You guys still hungry?"

"Hell yes!" Mott says.

He gets up from the table, grabs the percolator, and starts making some coffee.

Doc grabs a knife and sets the pie on the table. He slowly cuts it into quarters, and then makes two more slices to create eight perfect pieces.

"You should have just cut four pieces. Did Marie make that?" Doyle asks.

"Yeah, she did."

My grandmother taught my brother how to make pies. Every year for deer camp, Dave brings up at least a couple. Usually pumpkin or apple, maybe some type of berry. And not with the store-bought crust. He makes his own. A combination of what grandma taught him and some experimentation on his own.

"Who's Marie?" I ask, full well knowing the answer.

Mott responds, "That's Doc's wife."

"I assume it's the same gal that was your fiancée prior to moving up here?"

"You would be correct," Doc says as he rummages around the cabinet for some plates and forks. "Married twenty-one years this past July."

Mott lights the burner and places the percolator on the stove top. He sits back down as we wait for the coffee to start perking. The pie sits untouched, right in the center of the table, as we wait for the coffee to brew.

"That's wonderful! Any kids?" I ask.

"Yeah, five. Four daughters and a son. Oldest is a daughter, nineteen, and then I have another daughter who is eighteen, a son who is fifteen, and twin daughters who are eleven."

"Wow, you've been busy! Almost a half dozen."

Doc laughs. "Yeah, I guess you could say that! Do you have any kids?"

"I do. Three. The oldest is a boy, twenty-six, and two daughters, one twenty-five and one twenty-three. Been married for twenty-eight years. Gosh, that seems like a long time. Are any of your kids showing an interest in medicine?"

"Well, somewhat. My oldest is over in your neck of the woods at Aquinas College. I think she might end up in the medical field in some way, but I don't think as a doctor. My other daughter is a high-school senior, headed to the University of Michigan next year."

"She must be pretty smart," I say.

"Actually, both of them are. Jigger's planning on dental hygiene."

"That's her name? Jigger?" I say.

Mott, Doc, and Doyle all laugh.

"What's so funny?"

Mott says, "Doc's got a nickname for pretty much everyone."

"So her name really isn't Jigger?"

"No," Doc says. "Her name is Madeline."

So there it is. That's my mom. I'll be damned. A senior about ready to start college. I wonder if I can dig around for more information later without raising any suspicion.

"How the heck did you come up with Jigger?"

"Hell, I don't know. Just popped into my head, I guess. Anyways, my son Billy is at St. Lawrence Seminary in Wisconsin."

"He's going to be a priest?"

Again, Doyle and Mott laugh.

"That will be the day," Doyle says. "Kid's a prankster. Always building models just so he could put firecrackers in them and blow them up or set them on fire. Can you just imagine his sermons?"

"That sounds like fun to me."

I smile as I say that, thinking back to when I was a kid and we had a party at our house one Fourth of July. I might have been maybe twelve or so, and Uncle Billy was there. He grabbed a handful of sparklers and asked me if I wanted to make something really cool with them. So, we headed out to the garage and found a used model-rocket engine. He took a screwdriver and cleaned out the inside so all that was left was the thick paper tube. Then he took the sparklers, laid them on the workbench, and hit them lightly with a hammer to break them up into small pieces. Finally, he packed the tiny pieces into the tube. He took the tube and put it into the vise, and then lit the end with a match. When it ignited, it shot a stream of fire and sparks about two feet into the air. Scared the hell out of me! When it was done, I looked at Uncle Billy, and he had this mischievous look on his face I'll never forget. There was another time when my son was up here for deer camp, along with a couple of his friends. We had a big bonfire going, and Uncle Billy decided that he didn't want his La-Z-Boy anymore. He told the kids to go toss it on the fire. Those three boys couldn't haul it outside fast enough to torch it, with Uncle Bill laughing the whole time! Yep, he definitely was a prankster. I guess I can see why he didn't become a priest. Too much of the devil in him, no pun intended!

Now would be the time to tell them that Billy would go on to become a veterinarian—and a good one at that. He loved animals, and animals loved him. They recognized his kind heart and soft touch. We consulted him a few times when we had Zeus, our lab-retriever mix. We were up here one weekend, and

Zeus was laying on the floor right about in this same spot. He kept licking his paw. We had been out hunting all day. Uncle Bill gently lifted Zeus's paw and examined it while the dog patiently looked at him, and determined that he had plugged up one of his sweat glands. "He's going to lick it all the way home," he told me. He predicted it would blow up like a big blister and then pop, leaving a hole right between his toes. And sure enough, it happened just like that. I called him after I got home to confirm his diagnosis, and he told me to stuff it with Neosporin and it would heal just fine. It did just that. I have heard that Doc had the same bedside manner with his patients. Warm memories.

"Why you smiling at me?" Doc says.

His voice snapped me out of my thoughts.

"Oh, sorry. Just thinking about your son the prankster doing mass," I lied.

"Well, yeah, the kid does like to have some fun, but what kid doesn't. We figured the seminary might give him more structure. We wanted to get him into St. Paul's in Saginaw, but they didn't have any openings. He seems to be doing alright, but I'm not really sure that the priesthood is his calling. He does like animals—I know that."

"Well, maybe he can become a vet?" I try to catch myself, but the suggestion blurts out before I'm able to stop it.

"Yeah, that's an idea. He's got some time to figure things out, though, so no need to rush."

All of a sudden, Mott looks over at the stove and says, "Shoot! The percolator is bubbling! I didn't even know it started."

"It doesn't look too dark yet, Dad. Just give it a few minutes."

Doc says, "So, enough about me and my family. Let's say we try and clear some more fog from your memory. Tell me about your family. A wife and three kids, was it?"

"Well, hmm, let's see. My son is in LA, writing and trying to make it as a movie director, and both of my daughters just graduated from Michigan State and are considering graduate school for something in the medical field."

"A movie director, wow. How's that going?" Doyle asks.

"It's a tough row to hoe. He is a really good writer and has written several movie scripts, but he is also bartending to make ends meet. I sure wouldn't want to be in that business, but ever since he has been little, that's what he has wanted to do."

"So your daughters are considering graduate school? In what?" Doc asks.

"One of them in occupational therapy and the other in physical therapy," I say.

"What colleges are they looking at?"

"I'm not really sure, to be honest with you," I lie again. I probably need to say the minimum. Being a doctor, I'm sure he knows all about OT, PT, and which colleges in the nation offer these programs, especially locally. Some of the schools that have these programs in 2016 might not have had them in the 1960s.

"Those are both good professions. I work with them all the time at FOH."

"FOH—what's that?"

"Flint Osteopathic Hospital."

"FOH? I thought you said your practice was in Montrose?"

"It is, but I also see patients a few days a week at Flint Osteopathic."

Mott says, "Yeah, Doc's one of the founders there."

"Really?" I say. "That's great! How did that happen?"

"Right before I moved here, the hospital was just getting started. It was the first osteopathic hospital in the area. A few years later, they asked several osteopaths in the area if they would like to help the hospital grow, and we got involved. In 1946, they expanded to ten beds and became Flint Osteopathic."

I was born at FOH. Dr. Norbett, one of my grandpa's friends, delivered me. I remember going to FOH as a kid back in the seventies and seeing my grandfather's photograph hanging up on the wall with the other eleven founders. About twenty years ago, FOH and three other hospitals merged and built a high-tech facility in Grand Blanc called Genesys. Sadly, just recently, they finally tore down the old FOH building. Doc's oldest daughter would go on to become an OR tech and work at FOH after his death in 1976, later moving on to Genesys. Doc's grandson Joe, one of the twins' sons, would become a nurse and also work at Genesys. Doc would have been proud.

Mott gets up and announces, "I think the coffee is done."

He sets four cups on the table and pours coffee into each one. He then sets some cream and sugar on the table. We each put a piece of pie on our plates and start eating. It tastes awesome.

"This is really good, Doc. Tell your wife she did a wonderful job!"

"I sure will. She will like to hear that."

"So, Doc, are there any boys sweet on your two older daughters?"

Mott snickers. Doyle elbows him in the side and gives him dirty look.

"Go ahead, Doc. Tell him about Mickey," Mott says.

"For Pete's sake, Dad, he's a good kid."

"Who's Mickey?" I ask.

"Jigger's boyfriend," Doc says. "They have been dating for a year or so. He's at Ferris in his second year. Business school, I think."

"That doesn't sound so bad."

Mott says, "Doc has to chase him out of the house every once in a while. Keep the kid honest. Tell him about that one time when you got out of bed to take a leak and he was in the family room with Maggie."

"Oh yeah, that was a good one! It was about one in the morning, and I got up to go to the bathroom. I heard something in the front room, and there they were, sitting on the couch. So, I asked Mick how he wanted his eggs cooked. He told me that he liked them over easy."

Mott and Doyle burst out laughing. Doc just smiles.

"He doesn't get it!" Mott says, noticing my blank stare, pointing at me.

"I guess I don't."

Doyle says, "Doc was subtly telling him to hit the road because it's late! You know, so late that it's almost morning? I might as well make you breakfast!"

I smile, embarrassed by my stupidity.

"Interesting, I've told that story plenty of times, and you and Mick were the only two that didn't get it. Are you guys related?" Doc jokes.

All three start laughing again.

"Did he leave?" I ask Doc.

"Maggie knew what the hell I meant, so she told him I wasn't really making any eggs for him and that he should probably leave. So, he tucked his tail between his legs, hopped in his car, and took off. That split manifold on his fifty-five Chevy rattled the glass in every door and window all the way down the street. God those damn things are loud."

Mott and Doyle are really laughing now, slapping the table. Doc is just grinning.

"So, are they serious?" I ask.

"I guess as serious as you can be. I know that he wants to transfer to Michigan State next year, but I don't think his mom and dad are going to let him. They think he will be too close to Jigger."

"That's still a bit of a drive away. I don't imagine they would be getting into any trouble. Do you know his parents?" I ask, delving deeper into the abyss.

"Oh yeah. Our kids go to the same school and church. His dad owns a hardware store the next town over."

"What a coincidence," I say, looking at Mott and Doyle. "You guys know him?"

"Oh yeah. We know all of the guys over there. They have an International Harvester dealership, so they are a bit bigger. His dad, Kenny, is partners with his brother and a few other guys. They also go through Morgan Brothers, just like us, for their general hardware supplies," Mott says.

"Is Mick going to get involved in the business too, Doc?"

"I'm not sure. We haven't really talked about it. Wouldn't surprise me, though."

"Has he been up here with you to hunt?" I ask, not wanting to pry too much.

"Nope, not yet. I've thought about asking him, but the timing just hasn't been right, with him being at Ferris. I know he hunts quite a bit, you know—squirrels, rabbits, and pheasant. His parents have a cabin near Clare, and they deer hunt up there too."

Doyle says, "I'm sure he would fit right in up here."

I finish my cup of coffee.

"You guys mind if I have another piece of pie?"

"I was just thinking the same thing," Mott says, reaching for another.

Doc and Doyle grab the last two pieces.

"Good thing Marie made an apple pie too!"

I look at Doc. "No kidding? You have another pie?"

"Yeah, we can have that one tomorrow night."

We finish up the pie and take the last few sips of coffee. I look at my watch—nine fifteen. Doyle grabs the plates and forks, and puts them in the sink.

"You need some help with those, Doyle?"

"Nah, we can do them tomorrow afternoon. Doc's going to dirty a bunch dishes anyway for breakfast."

Doc chuckles a bit. Mott gets up and walks over to cabinet, and bends forward to read something on a piece of paper pinned to the side.

"Looks like eggs and bacon, with a side of hash browns. How about some toast, Doc? Got to have some toast with the eggs."

"You got it, Mott."

"What are you looking at over there?" I ask Mott.

"Doc's menu for the week. Pins it up here at the start of deer camp. The entire menu for the week."

"No kidding," I say as I get up to go over and take a look. Sure enough, each day, breakfast, lunch, and dinner. All detailed out.

I look over at Doc.

"A bit extreme, don't you think?"

Doc arches his eyebrows, and says, "Correct me if I'm wrong, but you didn't seem to be complaining too much about dinner."

Mott, still standing next to me, pats me on the back.

"He's got a pretty good point there, Michael Kenneth."

"I guess I shouldn't bite the hand that feeds me."

Mott laughs. "Mike made a joke! And on that note, I think I'm going to hit the sack."

"Yeah, me too, Dad."

Father and son head into the bedroom. I hear the strike of a match, and the ensuing hiss and soft pop of a propane light. I can see the shadows of Mott and Doyle moving around in the room.

"What time are you planning to get up?" I ask Doc.

"Around five. I'll get the coffee going first. We can start eating by five thirty or so."

I walk back over to the table and sit down.

"That's not too bad. What time do you try to head out?"

"Usually about six. Try to be sitting by around six thirty."

"You going out tomorrow morning?"

"Damn right. I'd like to shoot that buck that you and Charlie saw. You planning on going out?" Doc asks.

"I hope so. Unless my memory issues take a turn for the worse."

"Is it getting any better?"

"Not really."

"Not sure I should let you go back into the woods if you still can't remember how you got here. Do you even know how to get back to where you were hunting?"

I have to think about that one before replying. Everything looks different now. I guess I know the general direction, even if the woods is different. Just head to the east, and then to the south. I should be able to follow my tracks in the snow if it doesn't melt.

"Yeah, I'm pretty sure I know how to find my blind. Shouldn't be an issue. How about I hunt in the morning, and if things haven't changed, you can drive me to town and I can find a phone somewhere and call my wife. I'd rather not go to the hospital."

"Alright. I can agree to that."

Doc gets up and walks over to the Duo-Therm, adjusts the knob, and opens the doors a bit more.

"You hitting the sack too?" I ask?

"Nah, going to make a nightcap. A little something special. Would you like to join me?"

"Sure, I would like that."

Doc wanders over to the shelf and grabs a bottle. I wonder what he's going to make. Then it hits me again. Am I really here, having a conversation with my grandpa, who died forty years ago?

Doc turns around and grins.

"Don't worry—it's not tequila."

"Thank God! I think I've had enough troubles for one day."

CHAPTER 18

HOT TODDY

After some pouring, mixing, and stirring, Doc sits down next to me and puts two coffee cups on the table. The tannin-colored liquid steams and swirls upward in short tendrils.

"What's that?" I ask.

"Whiskey, honey, and water. Bedtime toddy. Put you right to sleep."

We both take a sip. It hits the spot, and smells wonderful.

"So, we got so busy talking about everything else, I never asked what you do for a living." Doc contemplatively sips his drink.

"I work for a company that makes rough-terrain forklifts."

"What's a rough-terrain forklift?"

"They look like, uh…"

I stop for a moment, remembering I have to be careful with what I say. They were constructed very differently in the sixties.

"…farm tractors. We flip the seat and steering wheel, and put a mast on it. They are used for agriculture, lumber, stuff like that—where you need a forklift to move materials over uneven terrain. It looks like you're driving a tractor backward."

"Oh yeah, I know what you mean. Aunt Jane's has one. It's an old Farmall."

"What's Aunt Jane's?" I reply, lying again, because I worked for them one summer in high school. Seems like I'm lying a lot tonight!

"They make pickles. Big operation over in New Lothrop, just south of Montrose."

"Ah, we have dealers in that area. In fact, our stuff is really popular over there. We probably sold them a conversion kit for their Farmall."

"I see. So, what do you do there at the tractor company?"

"I'm the chief operating officer."

"That's pretty impressive. How long you been there?"

"Almost fifteen years."

"Business degree?"

"Well, kind of. A master's degree in business, with an engineering degree."

I almost said MBA. I don't even know if an MBA existed in the sixties.

"That probably works well for your job. Oh, I almost forgot. I heard you tell Doyle you are from Belmont. Marie and I have been there a couple of times."

"No kidding. For what?"

"Golf. We are members at Saginaw Country Club, and a couple times a year, we compete at other country clubs around the state. We have played at the country club there, but the name escapes me at the moment."

"Blythefield?"

"Yeah, that's it! I shot really well there, and Marie took first place."

"Really? Is she pretty good?"

"She is, and also very good at bowling and tennis."

"Wow! Quite an athlete. Does she hunt?"

"No, but, she comes up here with me during bird season and goes out into the woods with me and the dogs. She's a great gal. We have fun together."

"That's really important, you know. I'm not embarrassed to say that my wife is my best friend. We like to do lots of things together too. She likes sports, and we like to hike, bike, golf, bowl, stuff like that. I still do things with the guys, though. And she and her girlfriends get together quite a bit. We have a good balance."

"Does she work?"

"Yeah, she does—a couple days a week."

"What does she do?"

"She's a physical therapist." I hear my own words and wince. That hot toddy let the truth slip right out of me. Now I need to think fast....

"No kidding! Why the hell didn't you tell me that before?" Doc blurts out.

"I guess it never came up."

"Where does she work?"

"Spectrum, uh...I mean, Butterworth Hospital in Grand Rapids."

I almost messed that one up. Spectrum didn't even exist in the sixties. Jeez, I'm going to have to be careful here.

"Sounds like your daughters might be following in her shoes," Doc suggests.

"Yeah, I guess you could say that."

Time to change the subject.

"How about Marie? Does she work?"

"No, she's pretty busy raising the kids, taking care of things at home. She does a great job, and I appreciate it. Hey, how the heck can you remember all of these details about your job, kids, wife, yet you can't remember how the hell you got up here?"

"Yeah, that is somewhat perplexing. Selective memory?" I reply, jokingly.

Doc raises his eyebrows.

"Funny you said that. Don't be offended, but that's what it seems like."

I look at Doc for a moment, trying to figure out the sudden change in direction. Is he starting to question my story?

"What you mean?"

"Well, you don't seem to have any issues recalling specifics about your family. And you seem to be able to carry on a conversation without any problem. Just seems like you're not telling the whole story."

I look down at my drink. It's gone, and so is Doc's.

"How about another drink?" I ask Doc.

"Of what?"

"Crown."

Doc grabs the bottle of Crown and fills my cup halfway. He looks at his cup for a minute and then pours some into his. We both take a drink, and then I look directly at Doc.

"Maybe I'm not telling you everything. Maybe I really don't have any memory issues, but I have a story that's so unbelievable, I'm afraid to tell you about it."

Doc's eyes narrow. "That's a bit disturbing."

"Well, maybe to you, but for me, it's more like a dilemma."

Doc pauses for a minute, stroking his goatee. "So what's the dilemma?"

"I'm not sure if I should tell you, even though I want to. And if I did tell you, I'm not sure you would believe me. But if you did believe me, I'm not sure where the conversation would go."

"That's a whole lot of uncertainty," Doc says, then takes another drink. "Why don't you just start talking, and let's see how it goes?"

Thinking about what I'm about to say, I look down at my cup, swirl the brown liquid a few times, then take a big gulp.

"OK. So when you came up behind me, by the tracks, what did you think I was doing?"

"You were on your knees, watching the train go by."

"I wasn't watching the train. I was looking under the train, to see the cabin."

"Really? Why?"

"Because it looked different than when I left it this morning."

"What do you mean, when you left it this morning? You weren't here in the morning."

Doc takes a sip.

"Yes I was. Walked right out of that same door about seven this morning and headed out to my blind. But the cabin was different when I came back, at least different from how I remember it. The woods was different. Charlie's house, too. A different car was parked outside. I should know what's different. I've been coming up here for years, and I know how this place should look."

Doc raises his eyebrows again.

"Now you have me worried."

"You're worried? Put yourself in my shoes. I feel like I'm in a dream—one that is very real. I've felt this way since I woke up in my blind and saw that monster of a buck. Have you ever had a dream that is so real you can't tell if it's a dream?"

"I don't know. I guess I've never thought about that."

"I think I have somehow traveled back in time," I finally say, relieved.

I take another long drink and notice that my cup is empty.

"Back in time?"

Doc pours more Crown into our cups.

"Uh-huh. This might be a crazy question, but is the year 1960? November?"

"It is."

"Then I've traveled fifty-six years back in time, to be exact."

Doc does some quick math.

"Fifty-six years. 2016? You came from the year 2016? You're insane!"

He just stares at me, brows furrowed.

"Seems pretty absurd, but yeah, that's correct."

Doc lifts his cup to take another drink but stops short and stares at me like he just thought of something.

"Do you remember the first thing you said to me when I walked up to you?"

"Yes, I do."

"Then you lied about not remembering it earlier."

"Yes, I did."

"Is it true?"

"I'm not sure. Maybe. Does that disturb you?" I ask my grandfather.

He stares at me, and I take sip. I was eleven years old when my grandfather died, so I never had any deep conversations like this with him. I wasn't even capable of it. And yet here we are, having a discussion that doesn't make much sense for either of us. It's probably worse for him, because at least in my lifetime, technology has progressed enough so that something as whacky as time travel might just be possible.

"Oddly enough, I'm not disturbed, but slightly concerned. I'm curious to hear more."

"I'm not sure how much I want to say."

"What makes you think that I'm your grandfather?"

I laugh.

"What's so funny?" Doc asks.

"I'm not sure what to say!"

"Well, you must know something!"

"OK. For starters, you look like him. The hat, the goatee, your profession, your wife, your kids, where you live."

"Well, that's not very convincing. Anyone could walk in here and tell me that with some coaching."

"You make a very good point."

"So if you're my grandson, who is your mom and dad?"

"Damn, you didn't waste time asking that one!" I reply quickly.

We both laugh.

"I'm not sure that I should tell you," I say, with sincerity.

"Why not?"

"Because you might use that information to somehow change something in the future."

"How would I do that?" Doc questions me.

"OK, let's say I tell you that one of your daughters is my mother. Or that your son is my father…"

Doc interrupts, "Well, I'm sure Billy's not your dad. Unless he marries a six footer! There's not a tall one of us in the bunch!"

We both laugh.

"Anyways, let's say that I tell you who my parents are, and you intervene in such a way that they never get married and have kids, which means that I wouldn't be born. I can't take that risk. It's like if you could go back to 1930 and kill Hitler, do you think the world would be the same as it is now? You could literally change history as we now know it. Only this time, it directly affects me."

"That's an interesting concept. I can see your point," Doc says, rubbing his goatee.

"I just don't know how to prove that I'm your grandson without the risk of screwing something up. You know, since we met, I have been worried about you finding out who I am, or who I *think* I am, and maybe it doesn't matter, because there is nothing that I can say to make you believe me. I mean, I could tell you something that is going to happen in the future, but that doesn't prove anything right now."

"You said that you left the cabin this morning. Was there anyone else up here with you?"

"Yes."

"Who?"

"My brother, one of Doyle's kids, his grandson, and a couple of our friends."

Doc laughs, then says, "No shit. Doyle's *grandson*? And what would be the names of all of these people?"

"Doyle's son, Tim, is one of them."

Doc stares at me while I take a drink.

"Well, just so you know, all of Doyle's kids are in elementary school, so I'm pretty sure they don't have kids."

I laugh.

"Yeah, I know that."

"How about your brother. What's his name? And Doyle's grandson?"

"I'm not sure that I can tell you that."

"Why not?" Doc asks.

"I guess because they don't exist right now, and I don't think it's a good idea that you know their names."

Doc starts to speak and then stops, as though he is searching for the right words.

"So, besides you and your brother, is anyone else from my family up there—here—or whatever you'd call it…?"

"No. Just my brother and I."

Doc looks at his drink and takes a long sip. He sets it back down and looks away from me. Is he thinking about Billy and why he isn't up there?

"Interesting stuff, but still not too convincing. Tell me something that only I would know that nobody else would?"

"I've been thinking about that, and nothing comes to mind," I say.

"Looks like you've got a bit of a problem then."

"Yeah, I guess I do. It's all so bizarre. I don't even know how to talk about it. By the way, speaking of people up here, where is Myron?"

"Myron?"

"Yeah, Myron. He's one of the members, isn't he?"

"Are you shitting me? Who did you hear that from?" Doc blurts out.

"Well, it's pretty much general knowledge," I say.

"Is *he* putting you up to all of this bullshit? This make-believe story about you being my grandson, somehow coming back in time to visit me?"

I laugh nervously. Doc is visibly upset.

"No. Why would I do that?"

"That son of a bitch has been begging us to make him a member, and we've been ignoring him. Don't get me wrong, Myron's a nice guy, but if you think I'm a bit particular, he's ten-times worse. The thought of him up here scares the hell out of us. We get a good enough dose of him back home, and the thought of bringing him up here is just too much. Mott would be ready to kill him in two days."

I have no problem visualizing that. I didn't know Myron that well, but I knew that he was one peculiar dude and could rub people the wrong way. I heard enough stories about that. I chuckle visualizing Mott attacking Myron, like an overcaffeinated spider monkey, fists in a blur.

"So, you think that Myron planned this whole thing just so he could become a member? How are you drawing that conclusion?"

"Well, he comes up with this crazy story about you, and then, at the right moment, has you toss in a little tidbit that he is a member. Get us thinking more about it one way or another. Move the process along. Actually, it's pretty clever. What's he paying you to do this?" Doc asks, glaring at me.

I can't help but to start laughing again.

"He's not paying me anything! He's not involved."

Doc gets up from the table, finishes his drink, and says, "Well, I think I've had just about enough of this bizarre conversation. I don't even know what to believe now, or even what to say, except I'm damn tired and ready to get some sleep."

"I'm sorry, Doc. I don't know what to say either, and I feel bad that the conversation ended on such a bad note."

Doc reaches up, turns one of the lights off, and heads out the front door to take a leak. I head into the front room and realize I don't even have a toothbrush. I turn back around and head outside to do the same, passing Doc coming back in.

"Lock the door when you come back in, and hit the last light, if you don't mind."

"No problem," I say.

Gosh, that sucked! I had such a great conversation going with Doc, and it all went to hell. I sigh and look up at the sky. Stars all over the place. I can see my breath, the vapor slightly illuminated from the light in coming through the window. I finish up and then head back in, locking the door behind me. I shut the valve on the last light in the kitchen and head into the front room. Doc is fiddling around the room in his underwear. I climb into my sleeping bag and zip it up. Doc turns off the propane light, and then I hear him getting into bed, with the sound of a zipper finalizing the process. Oh man, I really feel bad about how that ended. At least I figured out that I really can't prove anything, and on the positive side, he thinks this whole thing was concocted by Myron. I've got a scapegoat—Myron. I laugh to myself. It does sound like something he might do.

"Hey, sorry that I got a bit upset there," Doc says, after a few minutes of silence.

"Apology accepted. It's been a very frustrating day for me, to say the least. Hopefully, I'll wake up and find out this was one big dream."

Doc laughs.

"Yeah, me too!"

A few more minutes of silence go by.

"Hey, you're not planning on slitting our throats tonight, are you?" Doc asks.

We both start laughing.

"No, I'm just going to steal Mott's slippers and take your Caddy. By the way, where did you leave the keys? I'd prefer to not wake you up."

We both laugh again.

"Good night, grandson," Doc says sarcastically.

I smile in the darkness.

"Good night, grandpa."

CHAPTER 19

THE TRAIN (PART II)

I get out of bed and walk down the unlit hallway to the next room. There is a light on in the kitchen further ahead, but instead of going in there, I turn left toward the fireplace. I sit down at the end of the hearth, with my back against the glass slider, and pull my feet in close. I can feel the cold glass through the drapes, but it's countered by the heat coming through the register at the base of the hearth. I hear some rumbling in the kitchen now—pots clanking, cupboard doors opening and closing. I soak in the hot air and become more alert. The cat meows in the kitchen, and I hear someone speak. My mom. The roar of the electric can opener comes to life. More meows. I stare ahead, focused on the warmth.

"Michael, I didn't know you were up? How long have you been there?" My mom says, startling me as she appears from the kitchen.

"I don't know."

She walks over, sits on the hearth, and runs her fingers through my hair. She starts to cry, softly.

"Grandpa Doc died last night. He has been so sick, and his body just couldn't go on. I'm going to miss him so much."

I tell her I'm sorry, but a horn sounds while I speak, so she cannot hear me. I tell her again, but the horn interrupts a second time. I can see the sadness on her face, and I'm frustrated that she can't hear me. The horn sounds again, much louder, and suddenly I'm awake. It's the train! I was dreaming. I sit up in bed and look around the room. Light is flickering on the walls from the approaching locomotive's headlights. I take a deep breath and look over at the bed across the room. Doc and I are both still here. I gaze out the window and watch the locomotive go by, headlights disappearing, replaced by the roar of the boxcars as they rush past the cabin. Window panes shake. Glass rattles. Wheels click and clack over joints in the track, and I hear a squeaky boxcar wheel. I close my eyes again and take comfort in the familiar sound. Pacifying. Magical. I open them and look out the other window to see the headlights illuminating the trees in the distance. The train is not visible. There is only the light from the locomotive, speeding west—a black phantom with a searchlight, scanning the trees ahead. Eventually, the sound of the cars fades as the last one rolls by. I watch with anticipation until I see it, blinking red, in the dark of the night, progressing further away with each flash. Oscar! I watch until I can't see it anymore, then unzip the sleeping bag and head outside to relieve myself. Finished, I go back inside and climb into the bed. As I drift back to sleep, my thoughts return to that cold morning forty years ago in February 1976.

CHAPTER 20

DOC'S BREAKFAST

The sound of a mechanical alarm clock wakes me up. I visualize the blur of the hammer between the bells on the top of the clock. The sound echoes in the old schoolhouse. Doc groans and grabs the guilty party, its bells' noise deadened from his grasp. I hear a faint click and then the noise stops. Doc sighs and bed springs squeak as he gets out of bed.

"Do you need some help with breakfast?" I ask, sitting up in bed.

"Nah, I should be good. Just going to get the coffee going. You might as well just stay in bed until its ready."

Doc goes into the other room, and I hear the unmistakable hiss-pop of the propane lamp being lit. The boys stir in the next room over, and then the sound of a long, loud fart breaks the silence.

"Jeez, Dad, that was a nasty! You better go check your pants," Doyle says.

"Just wait until you smell it! I fluffed the covers, so it's drifting up. Here it comes! Can you smell it? Holy shit, this is really bad."

Mott starts laughing.

"Oh my gosh! It smells like a rotten pork chop!"

Both of them are whooping it up in the bedroom, howling with laughter. Pretty soon, I can hear sleeping bags being unzipped and feet pounding on the floor. Light suddenly reflects off the ceiling after one of the guys lights a lamp. Pretty soon they are shuffling into the kitchen with Doc.

"The smell is following you guys in here! What the hell, Mott, did you get into the garbage last night?" Doc says.

"I think it was that pork chop. It was percolating in my gut when I went to bed."

All three of them are laughing now. After a few more minutes in bed, I decide to get up and join them. Yellow-tipped, blue flames are dancing up the side of the percolator. Doc and Doyle are sitting at the table. I don't see Mott—or the toilet seat, for that matter. I catch a slight whiff of sulfur in the air and wince.

"Yeah, it stinks, doesn't it?" Doyle says, seeing me scrunch my nose.

"Yeah, just a bit. I'm impressed with how it lingered, though."

Doc chuckles, and says, "Mott's blaming me for it. Something about the pork chops."

"If you ask me, it was that beer he was drinking," I suggest with a grin.

"You're probably right."

Doc and I look over at the coffee pot, and liquid is splashing inside the glass ball on the cover. He looks down at his watch.

"Pull it at five fifteen," Doc announces.

I head outside and heed nature's call. It's still dark yet, and the snow still lingers. I look across the road toward Charlie's and notice they are up. I can see their shadows moving. I finish the task at hand and head back into the cabin. Mott's back from his trip to the outhouse, seated at the table.

"It's pretty cold out there," Mott remarks.

"Yeah, it is," I reply.

"It's a good thing that toilet seat was heated. It was so cold in there, the dump I left was steaming."

"Thanks for the details on that one, Dad."

I walk over to the window, and I'll be damned, the same thermometer that we have at the cabin is mounted on the wall. I didn't realize it was that old. Squinting, I can see the mercury level for both the indoor and outdoor temps.

"Twenty degrees," I say, heading over to the bench to sit down. We are all waiting for the coffee to perk.

"How did you sleep last night, Mike?" Doyle asks.

"Not too bad. How about you?"

"Real good. I never have any problems sleeping up here. Did you hear the train?"

"Yeah, I did. Actually, it woke me up from a dream."

"Good one or bad one?" Doc asks.

"Good one," I say, lying, recalling the events that happened forty years ago.

"Any naked girls in this dream of yours?" Mott asks, eyebrows arched high.

Doyle and Doc laugh.

"No naked girls, Mott. Sorry." I shake my head and then say, "It looks like Charlie and the boys are up. Lights were on, and I could see movement."

Doc says, "Yeah, they usually head out about the same time we do. I bet Charlie goes back out, too. They were probably up all night thinking about the big boy."

"You can't blame them. If that was the same buck I saw, I've never seen one that big—not only the size of the rack but the size of the deer. It was gigantic. Huge body, neck all swelled up. Probably an old, smart deer that lives in the swamp. Comes out in the fall to do his thing, then disappears for the remainder of the year. I'd really be surprised if any of us see him again."

"You said maybe a ten pointer?" Doyle asks.

"Or bigger."

The boys slowly nod their heads, eyes glassy, staring off into the distance.

"Coffee's ready!" Doyle declares, getting up from his seat.

He goes directly to the cabinet, grabs some cups, and shuts off the burner. He places the cups on the table, fills each with coffee, and then sets the percolator on the Duo-Therm. He goes into the backroom and reappears with some cream. Doc grabs some sugar from the cabinet.

"You guys have any Baileys?" I ask.

All three look at me with quizzical looks on their faces.

"What the hell is Baileys?" says Mott.

"You know, Baileys Irish Cream."

"Never heard of the stuff," Doc replies.

"Really?"

"Yeah, really. What is it?" Mott asks.

"Well, I don't know exactly. It's a whiskey-ish, liqueur, with some vanilla and chocolate added," I say.

"Where do you buy it?" Mott asks again.

"At a liquor store—where do you think?" I say, thoroughly confused now.

"You sure you've never heard of it, Doc?" Doyle asks.

"Nope."

Mott adds, "Hey, look, if Doc hasn't heard of it, it doesn't exist. The guy knows every liqueur known to mankind."

Frustrated, I wonder why they haven't heard about it. Baileys is pretty common. It must have been around back in the sixties. I stand up to go get my phone in the bedroom. I can just "Google" it.

"Where you going?" Mott asks.

"To get my…" Shit. I don't have a phone here! The internet wouldn't work anyways. I chuckle a bit, then sit back down. "… Uh, nothing, I guess. Something just popped into my head. What about some Kahlua? You guys heard of that?"

"Now that we have!"

Doyle gets up, goes into his bedroom, and returns holding a recognizable brown bottle with red lettering. He pours a generous amount into my cup and then adds some into his own.

"Thanks!"

"You're welcome."

We drink our coffee for the next five minutes, strategizing about the morning hunt. I learn that Doc and Mott hunt off Huckleberry to the west, and Doyle hunts on the east side, about the same distance in as me but further to the south. Actually, he might be near the same spot where my brother used to hunt, before they clear-cut the woods, forcing him to relocate across Huckleberry. Gosh, I hope that I can find my way back to my blind this morning. If we leave around six, I will be walking back in the dark, but I'll have my headlamp. Just can't let the guys see it, for obvious reasons.

"Well, let's get some food going," Doc says as he gets up and walks outside.

Within a minute or so, he appears holding some stuff in his hands, which he sets down on the counter. He grabs a large cast-iron skillet and goes to work on what appears to be hash browns. A stick of butter and some chopped onions go into the pan, along with the shredded potatoes. The smell of cooking onions fills the small schoolhouse. I get up, pour more coffee, add some Kahlua, and position myself next to Doc.

"Are those fresh hash browns?" I ask.

"Yeah, I did them the other day. Boiled the potatoes in salt water, then rinsed in cold. For some reason, it removes the raw potato taste. I also like to shred and season them before cooking."

Doc grabs another skillet, lights the burner, and starts cooking sausage patties. It all smells really good. I take a sip of coffee.

"Did you get the sausage at that meat place in Cheboygan?"

"Yep."

"They smell great. Hey, do you need a warmer-upper for your coffee?"

"Yeah, sure."

I grab the percolator and fill his cup.

"Hey, how about some of the Kahlua, too?" Doc asks.

"Sure," I say, adding some to his coffee.

Doc looks at me.

"So, how's your memory this morning?"

"To be honest, I haven't thought about it."

"Really? I would think it would be bothering you…" He says to me, with an astonished look on his face. My thoughts return to last night's confession and the bottle of Crown. Had Doc written off our discussion about time travel as mere "drunk talk"? Or had he forgotten our conversation entirely? Exactly how many hot toddies did we drink last night?

I laugh a bit and reply, "You would think so, wouldn't you?" He doesn't seem to be phased at all by last night's conversation.…

"Well, let's stay with the same plan today and head into town if things don't get better. I don't plan on hunting all day, so we can take a ride this afternoon when we get back in."

"Yeah, OK. You being a doctor and all, I guess I don't have much ground to argue with you."

I look down at the hash browns, and they are starting to crisp up with the butter and onions. Doc flips the sausage over with a metal spatula. Grease splatters during the process, dancing on the skillet like little volcanic eruptions. They are browned perfectly, just the way I like them.

"Hey, look, I don't want you to get all worried. You seem fine, and I'm sure that your memory will come back. Hell, maybe the trauma of seeing that big buck messed you up!"

We both laugh.

"Wouldn't that be something? Speaking of traumatized, would I be correct that the eggs are going into the sausage grease?"

"I can't think of a better way to cook them."

"I don't disagree, but I'm sure my arteries might!"

We both laugh.

Doc motions over to the cabinet.

"Grab one of those plates and some paper towels."

I place them on the counter next to Doc. He scoops the patties out and arranges them in circular fashion on the paper towels. The grease soaks into the paper almost immediately. I hear the crack of an egg and then the sizzle as it hits the hot grease. A dozen eggs go into the pan. Doc grabs a lid and places it over the eggs. He turns toward Mott and Doyle, who are still sitting at the table, drinking coffee.

"Doyle, do you want toast?"

"Yeah, sure. Thanks."

"You want some?" Doc asks me.

"Sure."

He puts the bread on the toaster rack and lights the burner. Then, he checks the eggs, replaces the lid, and gives the hash browns another stir, making sure to scrape the potatoes and onions sticking to the bottom of the skillet—the best part, if you ask me. Within five minutes, the food is on the table. Breakfast vanishes quickly, with small talk about the morning hunt. Mott finishes first and heads into the bedroom. Doc is up next; he grabs the toilet seat and heads to the outhouse.

"There is no worse feeling than being in the woods and needing to do that," I say to Doc.

"You've got that right. I'm hoping that those three cups of coffee will do the trick."

As I get up to take my plate and silverware to the sink, Doyle calls out, "Hey, don't worry about that stuff. Just leave it on the table, and we can take care of it later."

"Sounds good to me."

Doyle heads for the bedroom, and says, "Well, I might as well get dressed."

"Probably not a bad idea," I reply.

I look at my watch. Five forty. As I start to walk toward the bedroom, I can feel the urge coming on. It's about time. I know some guys take some toilet paper in the woods and do their thing when the urge hits, but I would rather walk a mile back to the cabin. Suddenly, I hear the door open behind me. I turn to see Doc putting the toilet seat on the hook above the heater. Thank God. I head over to grab it, and Doc smiles.

"I think the damage from Mott has dissipated. It wasn't too bad in there. A bit cold, though."

"Hey, I heard that," Mott says from the other room.

I walk through the door and then over several planks laid on the dirt floor, back to the toilet in the corner. It's not as nice as the one Uncle Bill and my brother built, but hey, it will do. I take a seat and scan through the magazines resting on an upside-down metal pail next to the toilet. *Popular Mechanics. Field and Stream. Outdoor Life.* Ah yes, *Playboy.* I pick it up and look at the cover. November 1960. I'll be damned. A girl with white gloves is making OK signs with both hands around her eyes, so they look like glasses. Wonder who it is? I start looking all over the cover for the hidden bunny head, but don't find it. Maybe they didn't do that back then. I flip through the magazine. An article about Edgar Allen Poe. Some nude photos. An article about Acapulco. I open the centerfold to take a look to see if it is someone familiar. Nope. Joni Mattis. Never heard of her. I'll have to Google her if I ever get home. I guess I could ask these guys about her. Finally finished, I head back in to get dressed. Doc is already in there, wearing hunting pants and a T-shirt.

"You all set?"

"Yep. One less thing to worry about."

We both continue to get dressed and are ready five minutes later. Wearing my black-and-red checked wool hunting outfit, I actually look like I belong in the sixties. Well, except for the orange hat.

"You really going to wear that hat? Mott might be right. You're going to stick out like a sore thumb."

I look at Doc.

"Well, you know, this is the type of stuff we wear in 2016."

Doc just stares at me, and a wave of recollection sweeps over his face. Then we both start laughing.

"Jeez, I forgot about that shit," he finally says.

I grab my gun and make sure that I have my knife, whistle, and wallet. I do a final sweep of the bed, and it doesn't look like I left anything, so I head into the kitchen. Doc follows, and we set our guns on the table, waiting for the others. Mott and Doyle finally appear, dressed and holding their guns. Motts has a little folding chair with a red fabric seat in his other hand. Doyle looks down at my rifle.

"What's that?" he says, pointing at my gun.

"Winchester, .308."

"What model? I've never seen one like that. May I?" he asks, wanting to handle the firearm.

"Sure, go ahead."

Doyle picks up the gun, and Mott sets his stuff down to get a closer look. Both of them are talking at the same time while examining the gun, and both seem bewildered. Doyle runs his hands gingerly over the basket-weave embossing on the stock.

"Where did you get this?" Mott asks me.

"It was my dad's gun. I shot my first buck with it about thirty years ago and have been using it ever since. Why do you ask?"

Mott looks at Doyle, and says, "It says Model 100 on the barrel. When did Winchester start making these?"

"I don't know. I've never heard of it," Doyle replies to Mott.

"I wondered the same thing the other day," Doc says to both of them.

All three of them shoot me a confused look.

"Are you sure this gun isn't some type of prototype?" Mott asks.

"I don't think so."

"Well, all three of us know our guns. Doyle and I sell them, and I am pretty damn sure we've never heard of a Model 100 Winchester," Mott says, looking directly at me, eyes narrowed.

"I, uh, don't know what to say. Maybe it is some type of one-off gun from Winchester, but my dad didn't tell me that."

Mott continues his questioning. "Where did he get it?"

"Hell, I don't know. I never asked him."

Doyle hands the gun to Mott and then disappears into the bedroom for a moment. After a couple more moments of examination and a few mumbles, Mott hands the gun back to me.

Doc changes the subject and suggests we get going. It's close to six. We head out the door, me first, followed by Doyle and then Doc. Mott turns off the last light and then walks out, locking the door behind him.

"You going to wear that stupid hat again today?" Mott asks me.

I laugh. "Yeah, unfortunately. Got to have something to keep my ears warm. Why? Do you want to trade me?"

Mott frowns at the thought of giving up his Elmer Fudd hat. "I'll pass on that offer."

We walk around the cabin and head south down Huckleberry. We notice that the lights are off in the Schweitzer camp.

"Looks like they're gone," Doc says.

We get about another hundred feet down the road, and I slow down.

"Well, boys, this is where I head in."

"Where about are you hunting, again?" Doc asks. "Just in case we need to come and find you."

Mott chuckles, and says, "Just look for that damn hat!"

Doyle nudges him, disgusted by his behavior. Seems like that happens quite a bit.

"About a third of a mile directly east, then south about the same distance, across the creek, and then back to the west about a hundred yards," I say, pointing in the general direction.

Doyle replies, "Yeah, I know where you are. I've walked back in that area several times. The creek flows to the west and into the beaver pond, right?"

"Yeah, that's right. I'm just to the east of the beaver pond."

"I've cut through there before. You have to be careful going across the pond. It's a bit mushy."

"So, you go in on the left a ways up, and you guys are on the west side of the road, right?" I glance at Doyle, and then Doc and Mott.

All of them nod.

"Well, OK. I guess I'll see you guys sometime around noon, or earlier if I get cold and don't see anything."

They agree to the plan, and then turn to continue walking down the road. I briefly watch them walk away and then duck under some tall pine boughs. Their conversation fades as I walk east along the edge of the woods.

CHAPTER 21

DAY TWO OF THE HUNT

Minutes later, I reach the entry point into the woods. I pull the headlamp out of my pocket and put it on. It is still dark, but the lamp helps me see where I'm going. Fortunately, there was snow on the ground yesterday, and I can see my tracks. Gosh, I was so freaked out I didn't notice that. The tracks should make this easy. Minutes later, my tracks turn to the south, and eventually, I am crunching through the thin ice on the creek. I walk south for another couple hundred yards, then to the west, still following my tracks in the snow. I look up and see the shape of the blind in the distance. It's still there, thank God. Moments later, I am unzipping the windows. I work my way around to the door, unzip it, and step inside. Setting my rifle up against one of the windows, I zip up the entry door and get myself situated. I take a peek at my watch. Six twenty-five. I get more comfortable and recall the events of the past twenty-four hours. Where do I even begin? Is this still all just a dream? It sure doesn't feel like it. Dreams feel fuzzy and unfocused, and this feels too real.

Gazing out of the blind and into the darkness, my mind starts to drift. Yeah, I just don't think a dream feels this real. Dreams always have this sense of not being true, even when you are in the middle of one. It's hard to explain why that's the case. Maybe there is some psychological term for it. But I know what I feel right now, and I feel like I'm stuck in 1960. A wave of panic suddenly hits me. Oh shit, Doc might take me to the hospital the next time I see him! What the hell am I going to do? Wait, what if I don't go back to the cabin? What if I just walk out of the woods, go into town, and try to get a ride back home? Then reality hits me: I don't have a home. A wave of warmth rushes over my body. What if I never get back home? What am I going to do? I slink back down into my chair a bit more and try to wrap my head around that thought. I will never see my wife and kids again. For the next few minutes, I just stare off into the distance, focused on the possibility that I might never find my way home.

The snow has stopped, and the lower eastern sky is a slight orange, which transitions to a dark blue above. I look at the time again. Five after seven. I stare into the orange glow, and it looks so beautiful. My eyelids feel heavy, and I sink further into the chair. I pull my hat down and bury my chin into my coat. I wonder what Judy is doing right now. Probably still in bed. What's today? Tuesday, I think. That's right—opening day was Monday. Yep, she's still in bed. Doesn't work on Tuesday. I laugh a bit. She likes her days off. Not the morning person is my wife, as Yoda would say. I chuckle again. A sense of comfort comes over me, and I sink further into the chair.

CHAPTER 22

A DREAM WITHIN A DREAM

The big yellow thing across the street is scary, making lots of noise and moving around a lot. Why am I so scared? I stare at it some more. It's my birthday today, and I'm four years old. I wonder what that thing is. And why is it across the street from my house? It scoops massive mounds of dirt out of a hole, and there is a man riding it like a horse. Even though I am scared, I'm curious, so I start to walk toward it. A car passes by, blaring its horn. I flinch. I am standing on the sidewalk, still watching the man with the yellow thing, forming giant piles of dirt. I start walking again, and another car goes past me, beeping its horn. I am now more terrified than ever, watching that thing make dirt piles. The man is waving at me. He stands up and waves more, so I wave back. Suddenly, I hear another horn blaring. I turn my head just in time to see something bright coming at me.

My body jerks, and I'm suddenly awake. I hear the sound of a train horn in the distance. Two long blasts and one short.

I turned four that day, on November 18, 1964, and all I remember is that backhoe digging a hole while I stood transfixed at my grandma and grandpa's house in Montrose. It's one of my earliest memories as a child.

It's getting brighter, and I look at my watch. Ten after nine. I must have fallen asleep for two hours! I look around to gain my bearings and notice that the woods still looks the same as it did when I walked in this morning. Damn. Negative thoughts creep back into my head. I decide that I can't go back to the cabin, so I start to formulate a plan. I could just follow the tracks into town. But I need to make sure those guys don't see me. And I should probably ditch the orange hat.

"Snap!"

I freeze as the sharp sound breaks the morning silence. There it is again.… "Snap!" And then a few more. I turn my head slowly in the direction of the disturbance. There! I see something! In the brush.

"Snap! Snap!"

A dark mass moves right toward me. This is no squirrel. After what seems like an eternity, a large brown body finally appears, about twenty-five yards away, with a huge set of antlers. That's him! That's the monster buck I saw yesterday! Slowly, I reach for my gun, which is still leaning up against the window of the blind. The deer doesn't sense me; his tail is down, wagging from side to side. He paws at the ground and urinates on the scraped earth. I count the points and see ten, maybe eleven. Holy crap, he's bigger than I thought! I start to bring the gun up. Quietly. Slowly. The buck turns and is now broadside. Suddenly, he stops and looks behind him. His ears perk forward, and his tail starts to slowly rise. Does he hear something? Another buck? After a minute or so, the tension subsides and he resumes walking. The cold wood of the stock is now against my cheek, and the safety is off. Crosshairs centered on his body, my finger rests gently on the trigger. He stops. I exhale slowly and pull the trigger. The gun kicks, with a loud report.

CHAPTER 23

LE SAUT EN ARRIÈRE

When a rifle recoils from a discharged round, the shooter's eyes reflexively close. You might not realize it, but it happens. In that fraction of a second, when the gun goes off, you blink.

After the shot, I expected to see the deer either on the ground or running away. I saw neither. In fact, what I saw was totally unexpected yet *expected*. It was the woods, looking just the way that I remembered it on opening morning. Immediately, I unzip the back of the blind and walk over to the area where I shot at the deer. No tracks. No blood. Nothing. What the hell? There should be tracks right here! He was standing in this exact spot when I shot. Dumbfounded, I look around for some evidence that I just shot a monster buck. How could I miss him? He was only about thirty yards away. I circle the entire area, about fifty yards across. Finally, I go back to the blind and sit down. I look at my watch. Ten in the morning, November 15. Still opening day. Wait a minute, I thought it was a day later? What happened to me? For the next thirty minutes, I try to recall everything that had happened since I walked out here this morning—or was it yesterday morning? Have I been dreaming for the last hour, or did I somehow actually go back to 1960 for a day?

Confused, I decide to head back to the cabin to try and make sense out of this whole ordeal. I notice there is no snow on the ground. Wait! There was snow on the ground when I came out this morning with Doc—that's how I found my blind! But wait, back home in 2016 we didn't have snow; it was frosty. Eventually, I reach the sandy area and cross the creek. Looking up, I see some bright orange about fifty yards ahead, and Kerry waves from his blind. After a short stroll, I'm standing next to him.

"You heading back in already?" Kerry asks.

"Yeah."

"I might as well go with you. My toes are pretty cold, and I was thinking about calling it quits in a half hour anyways. I haven't seen a damn thing out here. Did you?"

"You didn't hear me shoot?" I ask, bewildered.

"Huh? You shot your gun?" Kerry says, looking confused.

"Yeah, at a monster buck. Were you sleeping?"

"No, I've been awake the whole time. Seriously, you shot at something? I would have heard it. You're just over there," Kerry says, pointing to the south. "How big was it?"

"At least ten, maybe eleven."

"No shit! Did you see any blood?"

"I didn't find anything. No blood, no tracks, nothing. The weird thing was, right after I shot, he was gone. Had him right in my sights, pulled the trigger, and he was just gone."

"What do you mean, he was just gone?" Kerry asks.

"I mean *gone*. I never saw him drop or run off. He just vanished."

I can't believe what I'm saying. It doesn't make a damn bit of sense. Kerry must think I'm nuts.

"Just vanished? That's weird," Kerry says, eyes narrowed. "Do you want to go back and look some more?"

"No, I'm not sure how much good it will do. I spent about a half hour walking around the area where he was standing, and then walked out in a big circle looking for some blood. Nothing."

"You sure? I mean, we might as well keep looking."

"No, I'm not spending another hour looking for nothing. I guess I could have missed it. But I should have seen it bolt. So, you're dead serious? You never heard my gun go off?"

"Nope."

Kerry stands up, stretches, straps the gun over his shoulder, and walks out of the blind.

"Weird," I say.

We both start walking down the path.

"Did you fall asleep? Maybe you were dreaming?" Kerry jokes.

I laugh a little bit, then say, "Funny you should say that."

"What do you mean?" Kerry asks, studying my face.

I hesitate to answer, and we continue to walk down the path. Do I tell him? It was just a dream, right? What's the harm? Everybody has dreams. It never really happened, did it? No, because here I am right now. Just a dream. Yeah, it was just a dream—a very vivid dream.

"Actually, I did fall asleep and have a dream. That's what's funny."

"Really? What about?"

"Let's just say that I met Doc, Mott, and Doyle."

"Well, what's so weird about that? That's pretty cool," Kerry says, looking straight ahead as we make our way down the old logging path.

"Have you ever woke up from a dream and felt like it really happened?"

"Yeah, sure."

"This was different."

"How?"

"I'm not sure how to describe the feeling, I just know it was different than other dreams that I have had. You know, after you wake up, it's still in your mind, real fresh, and then they disintegrate, piece by piece, until you are left with just fragments. At the end of the day, you can't recall much of anything."

"That sounds about right."

"Well, this one's not doing that. I can still remember every detail of what happened."

"Fill me in."

For the rest of our fifteen-minute walk back to the cabin, I tell Kerry about my dream. Finally, we arrive. The others must still be out hunting. I remove the clip from my rifle and cycle the chamber to remove the cartridge loaded in the breech. It ejects and lands on the grass a few feet over. I grab it, snap it into the clip, and put it in my pocket. Kerry is doing the same thing but seems distant, his mind off processing everything I've just relayed. I reach up behind the shutter, grab the key, and open the padlock.

"Hell of a dream. You're right about remembering so much of it," Kerry says.

We are both in Dave's bedroom now, wiping our guns down and placing them in the cabinet.

"Yeah, I know. It still freaks me out, just thinking about it."

"You do seem a bit rattled."

We strip out of our hunting clothes and get into something more comfortable. Dressed in jeans and a flannel shirt, I grab some coffee and take a seat in the back room. Kerry soon joins me, mug in hand. I turn the propane wall heater control knob to the next highest setting, and the room begins to warm up. Kerry is looking at something on his laptop.

"You're not working, are you?"

He sighs. "Oh yeah, just a little bit. We have this big project going on, and unfortunately, a bunch of dipshits are on the team. None of them can make a decision for themselves, so they are always asking me for direction. It drives me nuts."

"That sucks."

The door to the cabin opens, and my brother walks in.

"Hey, you guys see anything?" he says.

"Nope. How about you?"

"Nothing, except some squirrels and a grouse."

He disappears from the doorway and heads to his bedroom to change out of his hunting clothes.

CHAPTER 24

THE TALE

"That's one heck of a story," Tim says.

"Yeah, I know."

"So, do you think you shot that deer in your dream?" Kerry asks.

"Well, I guess that's what happened. Did any of you guys hear a gun go off from the direction of my blind?"

"I heard a couple shots, but there were off to the north and west," Tim says.

"I heard a couple too, but they were more to the east," Kent declares.

Tim says, "We should ask Pete if his dad shot an eight pointer that morning. Didn't you say it was November of 1960?"

"Gosh, what if he did?" I say.

"It still wouldn't mean a damn thing. Even if he did, maybe you heard him talking about it some time ago and you just forgot about it. It was buried in your subconscious."

I swirl the whiskey in my glass, then take a drink.

"Well, what about the conservation officers that showed up to take a look at Charlie's buck?" I say. "I don't remember ever hearing about them. I mean, I can still remember the details of those two. The red hair, the chewing tobacco..."

"Well, I think that Pete's grandpa actually was a conservation officer, but it's the same thing. You probably heard Pete talking about them at some point. Or maybe there were some pictures of them that you saw the other day. Doc, Mott, and Doyle knew all of the Schweitzer brothers. They hung around here quite a bit back then. I'm sure that we talked about them. You just don't remember it."

"Yeah, maybe you're right," I say.

"Besides, how can you prove it really happened?" Tim says.

"Good question. I don't know."

"It's a good story anyways," my brother says.

"I guess," I say with some resignation.

My dream discussion gets old, and we move on to other things. Eventually, worn out from a busy first day, the group disbands and heads to bed.

Relaxed and zipped into my sleeping bag, I realize that I don't have my headlamp. I'll need it to take my inevitable trip outside in the middle of the night. Reluctantly, I get up and reach into my hunting jacket pocket. Not there. I check the other side. Got it! But then my hand touches something else— the gun clip. And I realize that I never checked the clip to see how many rounds were left. If I really shot that gun, I should have four cartridges, not five. Turning the headlamp on, I count the cartridges. One, two, three, four. I go back to my coat and reach in the pockets again. Maybe I put the ejected round into another pocket. Nothing. I check both pockets in my pants. Nothing. I grab the box of ammo and open it up. I know for a fact that two of the spots were already empty. I slide the foam insert out of the cardboard package. Seven empty spots total, including the two that were already there. I took five out, just like I thought. Where is that other bullet? I go back through all my pockets again, looking for it. Frustrated, I crawl back into bed. Did I actually shoot the gun? I quietly contemplate, and the sound of the train splits the silence off in the distance.

CHAPTER 25

MONTROSE, MICHIGAN, DECEMBER 1960

A short, barrel-chested man crosses State Street with urgency. He is wearing a long camel-hair overcoat, a brown Stetson hat with a zebra-print ribbon, and nice shoes. As he reaches his destination, he approaches another man holding the door open for him.

"Good morning, Doc," he says to the man in the Stetson hat.

"Good morning, Johnny," he replies. "Thanks."

"No problem. Enjoy your day."

"You too."

Doc walks toward the back of the store, headed for a counter manned by a person in a white lab coat.

"Good morning, George. How you doing?"

"Pretty good, Doc. How about yourself?"

"Not too bad, thanks. Hey, I had a gap in my appointments, so thought I would come over and see if those photos were developed."

"Matter of fact, they are. Just a minute."

The pharmacist disappears for a moment and then reappears with a package. He hands it to Doc and then punches some keys on the cash register. A bell rings, and the drawer springs open.

"That will be $1.50."

"Damn, sure is getting expensive to get these things developed," Doc says.

He reaches into his pocket for some cash, sorts out the correct amount, and hands it to him. George puts them money in the cash register and shuts the drawer.

"Yeah, I know. At least these are black and white. Color is worse."

Doc opens up the package and starts flipping through the photos.

"Got some deer camp stuff in there?" George asks.

"Yeah."

"Mott stopped by a few days ago—said that you had a visitor up there. Kind of a weird fella. Just showed up one afternoon, stayed with you guys that night, then flat out disappeared the next day. Said you guys spent some time looking for him but never found him."

"Yeah, that's about the gist of it. Nice enough guy, though," Doc says, still focused on the pictures.

"Mott said that he had some memory issues. Couldn't remember how he got up there or something like that? Also said that he called you 'Grandpa.' Is that true?"

Doc suddenly freezes, finding what he is looking for. He pulls the photo out of the package and stares down at it. He rubs the photo with his thumb, turns it over to look at the back, and then flips it back over again. He can't help but just stare at it.

"What's the matter, Doc? One of them messed up?"

Doc looks up, startled from his deep concentration.

"Huh?"

"You alright Doc? You look like you just saw a ghost!"

Doc puts the photo back into the pack, hands trembling. George notices that his friend is clearly distraught.

"I'll see you around George—I just remembered that I need to take care of something. Thanks!"

Doc quickly turns and rushes out.

George hollers, "Sure. See you later, Doc! Tell Marie hello for me, will you?"

Doc doesn't hear him. All he can think about is that photo. Black and white. Inside the cabin at Trout Lake, the Duo-Therm heater in the background. A toilet seat hanging in midair, no face inside of it or a body below it. Just hanging there, as if held by invisible hands.

CHAPTER 26

THE LETTER

As I pull into my driveway, the realization hits me that another year is almost over. I feel like this every year after deer camp. Thanksgiving is next week, and then the mad rush to Christmas begins. Get the tree up, hang the decorations, go to a couple of family get-togethers, enjoy Christmas, celebrate the start of a new year, and then it's over. The ultimate let-down. On to the next year. It happens so fast that it's sometimes hard to enjoy. I park the car, sigh heavily, and make the decision to unload later. The smell of beef stew hits me as soon as I walk into the house. I'm home!

"Is that the great Trout Lake hunter?" I hear Judy call out from somewhere in the kitchen.

She suddenly appears from around the corner, wearing a green apron, her hands clasped together in front of her chest.

"Hello Jude," I say, giving her a big hug and a kiss. "Man that smells good!"

"It's Aunt Margie's no-peek stew. Doesn't it smell yummy?" Judy says, smiling, proud of her work. I'm one lucky guy that she is such a great cook!

"Yes, it does!"

"So…did you guys catch anything?"

I laugh, but she doesn't realize why.

"Nope. None of us. We saw a bunch of does, but no bucks."

"Surprise, surprise. Did you have a good time?"

"Yeah, we had a great time."

"Who was all there?"

"My brother, Tim, Kent, Kerry, and Del's son, Dave. It was a good group this year—larger than usual."

"Where's your stuff? Do you want some help bringing it in?"

"I was going to get it later but, yeah, why not. Let's get it done. What I really want is a long, hot shower. It's been five days."

She wrinkles her nose and says, "You do smell a bit gamey."

"Gee, thanks."

Within short order, we both unload the car. I sort through my clothes, put the dirty stuff into the laundry basket, and leave the rest in the duffel bag to take upstairs. Looks like I took more than I wore, yet again. When will I learn? Judy sorts through the cooler and puts the remaining stuff back in the fridge.

"So, any good stories to tell?" she asks.

"Well…"

My tone registers instantly and her eyes grow wide. "What happened? Tell me!"

"Well, I don't know how good of a story this is, but on opening day, I fell asleep in the blind and had this really weird dream."

"That's it? A dream? You fell asleep in your blind and had a dream? That's your good story?" she remarks, expectations deflated. Her reaction makes me laugh.

"Yeah, a dream. But it was…different."

"How's that?"

"I seemed like it really happened."

"Huh?"

"It seemed real. I don't even know how to describe it, but you know how dreams are. You remember them right when you wake up, but then, almost immediately, you forget most of it. I still remember all of the details. I haven't forgot anything."

"Well, what was the dream about?" she leans in, again interested.

"I met my grandfather and a couple of his buddies."

"Doc?"

"Yeah. And Mott and Doyle Lehman."

She pauses for a moment.

"So, what do you remember?"

"I'm pretty sure that I fell asleep in my blind on opening morning. Next thing I know, something wakes me up, and I'm staring at this huge monster buck."

Judy laughs, and then says, "Yep, it was a dream alright. There are no bucks at Trout Lake!"

Damn, that's pretty good. I guess she pays attention to how many we shoot each year.

"So anyways, I'm about ready to shoot, and then suddenly, I realize that the woods looks different."

"What do you mean, 'looks different'?"

"Everything. The trees, grass, you know. I didn't recognize anything. I pretty much freaked out and panicked. Finally, I collected my wits and found a way out of there."

"If everything looked different, how did you know where to go?"

"Easy, actually. I heard a couple of cars, so I just walked in that direction. I finally popped out of the woods and could see the cabin—or something that looked like the cabin."

"Looked *something* like it?"

"Yeah, it was a yellowish color and still had the old additions on the front and back. It looked just like it did in some of those old photos. I was confused as ever at that point. Like I knew where I was, but I didn't. Anyways, I walked toward the road, and by the time I got there, a train was going through, so I couldn't cross. That's when I met Doc."

"Hah! What did he look like?"

"Just like the old photos, with his Stetson and goatee."

"Wow. What did you say to him?"

"I called him 'Grandpa.'"

Judy laughs, then says, "You called him 'Grandpa'?"

"I was waiting for a train to go through the crossing. It was loud, so he must have come up behind me while I was standing there. After it passed through, he said something and it startled me. The first thing that came out of my mouth when I saw him was 'Grandpa.' Then I passed out."

She laughs.

"You passed out while having a dream? That's a first!"

"I told you it was weird."

"So, what happened after that?"

"Well, I came to and he took me back to the cabin to check me out and make sure that I was OK."

"Check you out?"

"Yeah, blood pressure, heartbeat—you know, he's a doctor. Just as he was finishing up, Mott and Doyle walked into the cabin."

"Really? What did they look like?"

"Well, they both looked like they did in old photos. I mean, I knew Doyle, but Mott died before I was born. Doyle just looked younger. Doc introduced us, and then we went next door to look at a deer Charlie shot that morning."

"He introduced you to them? Who did you tell them you were?"

"Mike Kenneth."

Judy laughs out loud. "Mike Kenneth? Seriously? You used your middle name for your last name? You couldn't come up with anything better than that?"

"Yeah, Mott thought that was funny, too. But I didn't have time to think it through, you know! It just came to me."

"You were in a dream! It wouldn't have mattered what you said."

"Well, I wasn't sure of that."

Judy looks at me with concern, brows furrowed.

"You said they looked like they did in older photos. How old?"

"Like 1960 old."

"You think you were somehow in the year 1960?"

"I'm sure of it. I saw a 1960 calendar hanging on the door, opened to November. Doc was driving a fifty-nine Cadillac Seville that he said he bought the year before, and the cabin looked like it did in the sixties. Everything I saw looked like sixties vintage or older—the way people were dressed, the other cars that I saw, the packaging on the food they brought up, a *Playboy* magazine, even the train. The locomotive was one of those sleek, aircraft-looking F7s. They stopped using those before the seventies."

"Huh, this is getting pretty good."

"Anyway, we walked over to see Charlie's deer and then came back to the cabin. Doyle and Mott went back out to hunt, and I helped Doc make dinner. That's about the time that I made up a cover story about having some memory issues."

"Memory issues?"

"I had to do something, because I didn't have anywhere to go. Here I am, thinking that I'm in a dream, but what if I'm not? Doc actually suggested that I stay over at the old schoolhouse, so he could keep an eye on me. If I didn't get better by the morning, he was going to take me to the hospital."

"Was he worried about you?"

"I don't think so, or if he was, he didn't seem to be. I mean, I checked out fine, with no weird symptoms that anything happened to me."

"Hmm. So, what did you make for dinner?" She chuckles.

"Pork chops, yams, green beans, sautéed apples, cornbread, and pumpkin pie. And boy, he uses butter like Uncle Bill used to!"

Judy laughs again and says, "You remember all of that?"

"Every detail."

"Yeah, that is strange. Ten minutes after I wake up, I can't remember hardly any of my dreams."

"That's what I mean. It was the strangest dream I have ever had. Like I was actually there."

"So what else happened?"

"We played some cards after dinner, talked about this and that. Doc told me about med school, how he ended up in Montrose, and how those guys met. Mott told me how he ended up owning the hardware store in Montrose and how he met Doyle's mom, Macye. Stuff like that."

"That sounds pretty interesting," Judy says. "So, did they suspect who you are?"

"I don't think so. But Doc and I stayed up later, and we talked about our families and kids. He thought it was peculiar that I could remember so much detail about that but still not how I got up to Trout Lake—almost like I was lying about something. So, after a few drinks, I confessed that I thought I was having a very realistic dream and that he was my Grandpa. I didn't have much to lose at that point."

"No kidding! What happened?"

"Without going into much detail, I discovered that I couldn't really prove it to him. Funny, though, he did ask me who my mother and father were! I wouldn't tell him, and we both got a good laugh out of that. Then I asked why Myron wasn't up there with them, and he got really mad at me."

"Myron was their friend, right? The anesthesiologist. Why did he get so mad?"

"Because I thought he was a member, but turns out he wasn't at that time. Doc suddenly assumed that Myron arranged this whole thing, about me showing up with memory issues, so that they would vote him in as a member. You know, I ask Doc about Myron and plant the seed that he's a member, since I'm from the future? I guess Myron had been bugging the hell out of them about joining, and they were holding out. Anyways, Doc settled down a bit later when we went to bed, and he was fine in the morning. Then we had breakfast and went back out to hunt."

"So how did you wake up from this dream?"

"I was in my blind, and a deer came in. I'm pretty sure it was the same monster buck I saw the day before. Anyways, I brought the gun up to shoot, pulled the trigger, and in the blink of an eye, I was back to where I started. I guess the gunshot somehow jumped me back to the present."

"Or woke you out of your dream..."

"I guess. But it really seemed like I was there. So weird..."

"Yeah, it is really strange how much you remember."

"Oh, I remember more than that. I'm just giving you the meat of it."

"Wow! There's more? I can't wait to hear it."

Judy pours some wine in a couple of glasses, then asks, "Did you tell the guys about your dream?"

"Yeah."

"What did they think?" She asks, then takes a sip.

"I think they were entertained, and they gave me quite a bit of shit about it. Of course, they think it was just a dream."

"And you don't?"

"Ah, I don't know. I just don't know."

"So, are you freaked out about this whole thing?"

I laugh briefly, but Judy doesn't seem to find humor in her question.

"I don't know. Are you concerned?" I ask, suddenly worried about her expression.

"To be honest, I'm not sure. Should I be?"

"I guess not. I mean, I don't feel disturbed about the whole thing. But I've also had a few days to digest what happened and settle down. I guess I have come to the realization it was just a really vivid dream. I mean, what else am I supposed to think? That I really traveled in time, back to 1960, and met my grandpa and his buddies? That's insane!"

"I guess you're right. If you feel OK about it, then I'm not going to worry about it either."

Judy takes the lid off the crockpot and stirs the stew. The smell drifts, permeating the kitchen. I take a sip of wine.

"Why don't you take a shower, and then we can eat. I'm getting hungry."

"Sounds like a good idea."

Fifteen minutes later, I'm back downstairs, sitting at the table. A bowl of stew is steaming in front of me, and Judy is taking some biscuits out of the oven. There are some envelopes arranged on the table next to my bowl.

"Do you want more wine?"

"Yeah, thanks."

She partially fills both glasses.

"Some birthday cards arrived while you were gone. One is from your mom and dad. Do you think there's a little blurb about the day you were born?"

We both smile as I grab the letter.

"Oh, I'm sure there is. Let me guess...Dad speeding in Doc's Lincoln because Mom's in labor. Cops pull him over. He can't figure out how to get the power window to go down...."

"You have to admit, it's a classic story," Judy says.

I open the letter and pull out the card. Inside, there is another smaller envelope. It looks old, with yellowed tape on the back flap. On the front, written in script, are the words *For Michael*. Hmm, that's interesting. This doesn't look like Mom's handwriting, but it seems familiar.... I set the envelope down and look at the front of the card—a cabin in the woods, snow on the ground, and smoke curling from the chimney. I open it. As expected, written on the left flap, is a synopsis of Mom's day in labor, Lincoln and all. Then, something else...

> *PS—Enclosed is a letter from Grandpa Doc. He gave it to me about a month before he died, with explicit directions to give it to you after your fifty-second birthday. That's why your card is late! Sorry! Let us know what it's all about—we have always wondered!*

"What's this?" Judy asks, picking up the older envelope.

"I'm not sure. I guess Doc left it for me."

I hand her the card, and she passes me the old letter. I wonder what it is. There is something stiff inside. I turn it over and pull at the old, yellowed tape. It comes right off—no adhesive left at all. I open the envelope and pull out a handwritten letter.

Dear Michael,

The memories of the last few days are undoubtedly very fresh in your mind, and I hope that they continue to be just as vibrant for you as those memories have been for me for the last sixteen years. I pray this letter helps explain the last couple of days and gives you confirmation of your sanity. Or, possibly, you will just have more questions that cannot be answered. Either way, as time goes on, you should find comfort in what happened and, possibly, some closure. I certainly found closure, in time. I never could explain or understand it, but somehow we shared a very special moment during a very small slice of time in our lives.

A few days ago, you probably thought you were dreaming. Rest assured, you were not. After our brief meeting over the course of those two days in November of 1960, a string of events happened that turned your dream into reality for the both of us. I am so relieved that I can finally share this with you, via this letter.

Heading out to hunt that morning, I had no idea that I wouldn't see you again. Later, after we heard a gunshot, Doyle and I went to investigate. It was easy to find you—we just followed your tracks in the snow. However, when we got there, you were gone, and the only thing remaining was a single .308 shell casing. Doyle and I were dumbfounded, but Mott was skeptical and figured that you got your memory back and hightailed it out of there. He went to his grave thinking you were going to rob us, which was a good thing, since I don't think that he would have been able to comprehend what Doyle and I later discovered—that somehow you were actually there.

"Hey—what is with this picture?!" Judy asks. Her voice raises and cracks as she hands me a black-and-white photograph.

It's a photo of a man holding a toilet seat up in the air, with his head poking through the hole. I'll be damned—that's me! It's the picture that Doc took. On the bottom of the photo, stamped from the manufacturing process, is *November 1960.*

"Did you see the date? It says 1960!" Judy says.

"I do."

"When did someone take this? It looks so old. Is this some kind of joke?"

"You're not going to believe this, but he took it when I was there."

"Who took it? Doc?"

"Yeah."

"You mean, in your dream he took it?"

"Uh-huh."

"Is that the letter from your grandpa?" Judy asks, obviously having read the birthday card from my mom.

"Yeah, it is."

"Can I read too? This is unreal."

"Sure."

*Enclosed is a photograph. Do you remember me taking it? For the first four years, that photo baffled me! Doyle was the only other person I showed it to. I damn near looked at it every day, utterly perplexed. I **knew** you were in that photo when I took it. But, regardless of what I knew, the toilet seat hung in mid-air, as if held by the hands of an invisible person—until that day in November 1964, the 18th, the day you were born. I came home that evening from the hospital, and when I opened the drawer to put my watch and ring in there, I noticed the photograph was different. You were now there, in the photo, holding the seat, just like I remembered!*

I have to also mention your gun. The three of us were pretty confident that Winchester didn't make a Model 100, and sure enough, Doyle and Mott confirmed it when they got home. However, to our surprise, Winchester rolled out the Model 100 the following year, with a basket-weave stock option, in 1964. Several years after that, your father purchased a Winchester Model 100, in .308 caliber. It had a basket-weave stock, and the same exact serial number that Doyle remembered from your gun....

I stop reading and think about Doyle. He knew what happened, between the gun, the photo, and everything else. He saw what I looked like as I grew up. That explains why the times I spent with Doyle as a young adult felt like mentoring sessions. Not like how a father would mentor a son, but how a grandfather might mentor a grandson. Gentle, kind, like someone with years of wisdom. He *knew* what had happened and was trying to be there for me, since my grandfather couldn't. Judy nudges me, snapping me out of my trance.

"Do you believe any of this?"

The lump in my throat prevents me from replying, and I continue to read.

I wish that I could go back and see you again. How wonderful our conversations would be! But I'm glad that you didn't tell me all the things that you knew. Would I have lived my life differently if you would have told me? Would I have made different decisions? Probably not.... I came to the conclusion that it wouldn't have mattered, because our paths in life are predetermined, long before we are born, and try as we might, our destiny stays the same.

So, here I am now, with little time left to live. I shall dearly miss watching you grow up and experience life, and I'm sorry that I will not be there when you get married and have kids. I hope that your grandmother, Marie, will live to enjoy our family for a very long time. Maybe you will think about me once and a while? I would like that. Also, thank you for sharing about your wife and kids, even if it wasn't much. You seem very happy, which warms my heart.

I would like to give you some words of wisdom, but I'm not sure that I have any for you. Some would say that I have led a selfish life, and in support of that statement, they are probably right. I have not prepared for this moment in many ways, as you surely know. But I do find solace that I lived life to the fullest, discovering something enjoyable each day, and loving the ones

I was with. It's something you should consider. Life is short, with many twists and turns. Enjoy them fully, the good and the bad! Take care, grandson, and I look forward to the day we meet again.

Love,
Grandpa Doc
January 12, 1976

P.S. Michael Kenneth...Very creative! I realized the irony later...

Tears running down my cheeks, I set the letter down. I can't believe what I just read. It wasn't a dream. I really did go back in time and meet my grandfather!

"This is unreal, this is unreal," Judy says, grabbing my arm. "Do you know what this means?"

"Yeah, I do."

She starts to cry and hugs me.

"For obvious reasons, we can't tell anyone about this," I whisper in her ear, shaking with shock.

She pulls back from our embrace, smiles, and kisses me.

CHAPTER 27

EPILOGUE
NOVEMBER 13, 2017

Tired from the four-hour drive but excited to be back, I pull into the grass driveway. Lights are on in the cabin. I park the car by the steps, so that unloading will be quick and easy. Four other vehicles are parked on the grass, and it looks like Pete mowed. I get out of the car, and take a deep breath. The stars are so bright up here. I wonder if snow is in the forecast. I laugh a bit. I didn't even look to see what the weather was supposed to be like. Who cares? It doesn't matter—life is good! Feeling a sudden burst of excitement and energy, I head inside. Everyone is in the back room. Same group. They all beat me up here again.

"Hey, you finally made it!" my brother says, getting up from his chair.

"Yeah, finally. The drive seemed longer than usual, even though traffic was light."

I take my coat off and grab one of the available seats. There is a large box on the floor in front of Tim. It's open, with something sticking out of it.

"What's that?" I ask.

"Well, we were waiting for you to get up here so we could ask you," Tim says.

"What do you mean?"

"Show him, for Pete's sake!" Kent blurts out.

Tim reaches down and pulls out a huge set of antlers. It's just a simple mount, horns only, on a piece of wood. The center piece is covered with green velvet.

"Where in the hell did you get that? What is it, a twelve point?"

"My dad left it. Eleven points, I think, if you count this small one here."

Kerry says, "Yeah, we could hang a ring on it, so pretty sure it counts as a point."

"Doyle shot that?" I ask, surprised.

"I'm not really sure," Tim says.

"What do you mean, not sure?"

"Well, a week before coming up, I get this call from the law firm that handled Dad's estate after he died. They said they had a package for me. Been keeping it for years. My Dad wanted me to have it at just the right time."

"What do you mean, just the right time?" I ask Tim. The reality of the situation begins to hit me. Could it be? Suddenly, a wave of panic sweeps through me.

"Evidently he wanted me to receive the package this year. Right now."

"Well, that's pretty weird. How long has he been holding on to it, and why?"

"Hell, I don't know. The antlers were in this box, along with a note and a .308 shell casing."

".308 casing?"

"Yeah, and a note."

"A note?"

"Yeah. It just says, 'Ask Mike Jr.'"

Everyone stares at me as I get up, walk over to Tim, and take the rack from his hands. I run my fingers over the tines. They are rough and ridged. I've seen this rack before. The monster.

I look at the back of the mount and see something written in pencil: *MK. November 16, 1960.* I sit back down and take long, deep breath.

"So, what the heck is going on?" Tim asks.

The room is silent, except for the radio playing an Eagles tune, "Take It Easy." Everyone is waiting for my answer.

"If you don't have a drink, you'd better get one. You're not going to believe what I'm about to tell you," I say.

I reach into my back pocket for the letter and black-and-white photo.

Made in the USA
Lexington, KY
01 December 2019